AN ORIGINAL NOVEL

PIGGY™

INFECTED

by
TERRANCE CRAWFORD
and
DAN WIDDOWSON

Scholastic Inc.

There had once been an island called Lucella. Far past Doveport and somewhere south of the North Sea, its outer edges were sprinkled with long beaches and stretches of picturesque mountains that led to a salting of dense forests. The breeze off the North Sea meant there was often a chill in the air. It wouldn't have been out of place to see the residents of the island bundled up in jackets or scarves on their way to the Metro station. But that was then. That was before the Infection. If there were stars in the sky above the city of Lucella this evening, you could not see them. A dense mist hung above the island, blanketing the entire city in a thick layer of fog. The wind tore through the

trees, making a distinctive howling sound and causing Ben to pull his hoodie tighter around his shoulders. He considered calling it a night, then and there. These last couple of weeks, he'd had his fill of jump scares. To anyone else, the house in front of him was just like any other on the block—three levels, picket fence, a closely manicured lawn. To Ben, this was his best friend's house, and the last place Ollie had been seen.

Ben wondered if it was too late to turn back and go home. It wasn't as if there was much waiting for him there, either. He had lost track of his own family a while back. He hoped that they had made it off the island before it had locked down. There were dozens of safe spaces across the island, and Ben was confident that the grown-ups could take care of themselves. But Ollie . . . Ben was all Ollie had. Ben felt a rush of chills go down his spine, completely unrelated to the strange weather they were having. It seemed like just a few weeks ago, everything had been so normal, and now ... Well, now this. Ben shook his head, clearing the spookier of his thoughts and steeling himself for the task at hand. The aging brown wood of the picket fence creaked eerily as Ben pushed his friend's gate open, walking purposefully toward the front door. He had made this journey a thousand times before; why did it seem so sinister tonight? Ben traipsed up the front steps, reaching out to knock gingerly on the mahogany front door, which loomed much larger than he seemed to remember. His knuckles rapped on the wood, the sound seeming to echo across the empty street. The hairs on the back of Ben's neck stood on end. He had gotten used to making as little noise as he could.

"Ollie?" Ben cried out in a half whisper, not wanting to attract any unwanted Infected attention and not sure himself if he was expecting an answer. "It's Ben!" Again, this was silly. He had known Ollie since they were both in diapers. "No one's seen you! With everything that's going on . . . I'm worried about you." No response. Ben jiggled the handle of the door in vain, but it was firmly locked. He couldn't blame Ollie's family. The more he heard about the infected citizens of Lucella, the more Ben wanted to lock his doors and hide, too. And if that was what they wanted to do, they were more than welcome to—as soon as Ben made sure that Ollie was safe. He cupped his hands and called his friend's name. Again, no response. Ben sighed in resignation. This marked the beginning and end of his ideas. Surely if Ben could get inside, he would find some trace of Ollie, some clue as to where his friend had disappeared to. Of course, the front door wasn't the only way to get inside the house.

Ollie's house had always had the biggest windows in the neighborhood, and Ben was certain he had seen a good-sized rock on his way over here. Normally it was important to respect other people's property, but things hadn't been normal in Lucella for weeks. Skipping down the steps of the front porch, Ben made his way across Ollie's front lawn and down the street he had come from, back toward his own house. In another neighbor's yard, a collection of rocks led up to their front porch. Ben would only need to borrow one for this job. Pocketing a smooth stone, Ben made his way back up the street to Ollie's house. Ducking behind a parked car, Ben took in his surroundings, making sure that no one was around. The infected citizens of Lucella were one thing, but nosy neighbors were a whole other can of worms. The street was illuminated by only the dull, buzzing shine from the overhead streetlamps. Chills shot over his whole body again, nerves causing Ben's fingers to tremble. If Ben's parents had been around, they would have certainly disapproved of his plan. No, this wasn't just nerves. Ben couldn't shake the feeling that he was being watched. That was when he saw it.

Now that he had seen it, Ben was actually baffled that he had been on the lookout. It had snuck up on him, but it wasn't exactly inconspicuous. Twice his height and bearing down on him quickly was one of *the Infected*. Ben didn't know how to explain it, but the people of Lucella had started acting

strangely recently. For what seemed like no reason at all, large swaths of the population had recently become violently ill, and the ones who recovered . . . they were different. People were saying it was a sickness, an Infection, but others weren't so sure. Whatever it was, it was turning the regular people of Lucella into monsters. The Infected weren't worried about manners or hygiene; they only obeyed their base instincts to feed and to attack. And now Ben was face-to-face with one.

The creature made a distinctive grunting sound as it raised its arms, brandishing a metal wrench. The Infected was at least eight feet tall, dressed in an ill-fitting tattered red shirt. Its skin was pale and swollen, like it had been left in an inflatable above-ground pool overnight, and it smelled like a breakfast restaurant's sink that hadn't been cleaned in weeks. Ben's every instinct screamed out at him to run, but his legs wouldn't listen, and he found himself paralyzed by fear. The infected Pig Creature roared again, its eyes bloodshot and glowing red, its smell almost overwhelming this close. Ben threw his hands up reflexively to defend himself, the rock skittering across the pavement. The noise distracted the Pig, and it turned its head to follow the new sound. This was Ben's chance. He couldn't overpower the infected Pig, but if he got away, maybe his search for his friend would not be over before it began. Ben tried to control his breath as he forced his legs to obey him this time. He scrambled to his feet, allowing himself a small whoop of victory. He couldn't believe he had managed to overcome his panic. Just one more thing he would have to tell his family and Ollie once he found them. If he could beat one of the Infected by himself, then he could—*THWACK!* Ben's reverie was interrupted by a single blow from the creature's wrench. Ben fell to the ground, his head spinning.

Ben didn't know how much time had passed when his eyes fluttered open. He groaned in response to the throbbing on the crest of his skull. Naps were not high on the list of things you should have after a head injury. The constant hum and broken-down fluorescence of the streetlights had been replaced by the warm glow of a table lamp, and the biting chill of the North Sea's wind on the street had been replaced by the warmth of . . . a home? Ben sat up, his head aching, almost as if to remind him that he had been assaulted by a wrench-wielding Pig. As if he needed reminding. Ben stood up carefully, regaining his footing. He had never been in such close contact with one of the Infected before. He hoped he would never have to be that close to one again. What in the world was that thing? It looked so familiar, and yet Ben had never seen anything like it before. But he had seen this furniture. This room. Ben had been in this house before. He groaned as he gingerly touched his fingers to the knot growing on his head. Ben had planned to use one of the stones from down the street to smash in a window, then crawl in and search the house from there. Aside from the massive splitting headache, getting pignapped had turned out to be a much simpler way to get inside Ollie's house. But why had the Pig Creature attacked him, and more importantly, how did the Pig Creature get inside? Ben had an idea, but he pushed it to the back of his mind. He didn't want to consider that right now. His head throbbed again in the spot where his skull had been introduced to the infected Pig's wrench. It certainly wasn't pleasant, but Ben figured he would be okay. He opened the bedroom door, peering down the hallway for any sign of the creature.

In a lounge chair in the middle of the living room, the Pig Creature slept soundly. At least, that's what it looked like to Ben. Its massive head hung over its chest as it took labored breaths. Ben had no idea how long he had been out, or even what time of day it was. Ben looked past the slumbering Pig Creature to the front door he had been on the other side of not so long ago. He could make a break for it right now. He might not have anything to show for it, but he would make it out with his life, and a story to tell. Across the hall, even closer than the front door, was Ollie's room. Ben weighed his options. He could run for the exit, head home, and try again some other time when he wasn't nursing a probable concussion. Then again, wasn't this why he had come here to begin with? Hadn't his goal been to find something in Ollie's house that would help him track down his friend? What if Ollie had left a note, a calendar date, anything? If there was even a chance that Ollie had left a clue, Ben couldn't risk missing out on something like that. Before all this, Ben's parents had always told him he was hardheaded, but even he didn't think his head could take any more whacks. It was now or never. Putting as little weight as he could on each foot, Ben tiptoed across the hallway, every step causing the floor of his friend's house to creak a little too loudly for Ben's liking. It was torturous. One wrong move could wake the infected Pig Creature, and Ben didn't know much, but he knew that he wasn't up for another bout with the Infected so quickly. After what seemed like an eternity of sneaking across the hall, Ben reached his friend's room and quietly turned the doorknob.

Ben sighed in relief as the latch clicked and the door gave way. He never thought that he would be thankful that his friends didn't lock their bedroom doors. Ben closed the door behind him, making sure the click of the latch was silent as his relief turned to sadness, now facing the fact that his friend might actually be gone. Or worse, maybe he was one of them. Ollie's room was exactly as Ben remembered it—the bed, dresser, and chairs arranged in the same way that they always had been. If Ben didn't know any better, he would have thought that it was just another day after school.

KRRRSSH!

A faint, sharp crackling sound pierced the silence of the room. Ben's heart dropped to his stomach, and he thought for a second that the Infected had woken from its sleep and found him. No—it was just one of Ollie's walkie-talkies. For a few months, it had been all he talked about, though, like many fascinations, it eventually fell to the wayside. Unless . . . Ben extended the antenna of the walkie-talkie, holding the transmission button and clearing his throat. "Ollie, are you there? This is Ben. Over." Ben screwed his eyes shut tightly as he released the transmission button. If Ollie left this walkie-talkie behind, it would make sense that he had taken the other one, right? Ben's mind raced with a thousand different scenarios as he waited for a response. He was greeted with nothing but the cold static of a dead line. Ben shoved the walkie-talkie into his pocket. Maybe his friend was just out of range. At the very least, maybe the batteries would come in handy later.

Ben stood, looking over Ollie's room once again for anything that could help lead him to his friend and anything he could use to get past the drowsy monster currently occupying Ollie's father's favorite armchair. Ben sighed. There was not much to go on in either department. His eyes flitted across the room, taking in as much detail as he could before a glint of metal caught his gaze. He crossed the room to the desk in the corner of Ollie's room, picking up the shining metal and holding it to the light. Ben would recognize that chain anywhere—he had seen it hanging off Ollie's backpack every day since they had been old enough to walk to school . . . Ollie's house keys. Why would he leave home without those?

The walkie-talkie, the keys left behind . . . Everything that Ben found led only to more questions, no answers, and one very literal headache so far.

Ben wouldn't find any more clues here, he decided. He had been relatively lucky, but he was no detective. If he was going to find his friend, he would need help, and he would find no help here. He snuck out of Ollie's room, making sure that he had Ollie's keys and walkie-talkie before gingerly shutting the door and keeping an eye on where the infected Pig should have been. Should have been. Ollie's father's favorite armchair was now empty, the shape of the sleeping Pig still impressed in the upholstery. Ollie's father would not be pleased about that. Ben walked quickly toward the door, hoping to leave this place behind as quickly as he could. He would not be so lucky.

Ben heard it before he saw it; the distinctive grunting sound it made was almost porcine in nature but somehow scarier by multitudes. The creature stiffly raised its arms, making Ben wonder how something so big and clumsy had ever managed to get the jump on him in the first place on an empty street with no obstacles. The creature swung its wrench like a club. It missed this time, taking a moment to steady itself as Ben ran the length of the living room to get around it. The infected Pig gave chase, one of its eyes glowing red against the darkness, focused only on Ben. It swung again as it moved closer, intent on relieving Ben of his consciousness once more. Another missed attack as Ben took cover around a corner.

The Infected roared, looking around wildly for Ben. The thing had seemed to lose sight of him. Confused, it lumbered around the room before exiting to the kitchen. This was Ben's chance. He darted for the front door, tearing it open. He was so thankful to be greeted by the cool rush of night wind, Ben almost did not notice that he had been spotted once again. The infected Pig moved toward Ben with a purpose—whatever the Infected were, they did not like losing sight of their prey. The Pig moved up on him, stiffly raising its wrench once more. The Infected were quicker than they looked, but then, they would have to be. Ben slammed the door in the creature's face, pulling Ollie's silver-ringed keys out of his hoodie pocket and thrusting them into the lock and twisting them. The infected Pig roared on the opposite side of the door, realizing what Ben had done, now trapped . . . Maybe some time alone with its thoughts would do the infected Pig well. The angry oinking on the other side of the door seemed to indicate that the creature disagreed, but Ben couldn't help but smile. He had escaped. Maybe he was kind of good at this. A loud thudding on the other side of the door brought him back to reality. The Pig Creature may not understand how a door worked, but it might figure out another way to get to him eventually. He scurried off Ollie's porch and back down the street.

Ben pulled the walkie-talkie out of his jacket pocket, trying the obsolete device a few more times as he walked down the street, going nowhere in particular. If this cheap plastic two-way radio was the only chance he had of finding his best friend, then he was going to keep trying until someone answered or the batteries gave out, whichever came first. "Ollie, this is Ben, come in," Ben groaned wearily into the mouthpiece. "Come in, Ollie, this is Ben. Over." The same unsettling static followed each of his attempts, punctuating his failures with a dull crinkle. Ben's legs felt as though he were dragging them through molasses. They were beginning to feel the effects of walking all over the city. Finding a nearby patch of grass, Ben sat down, just to rest for a moment. He let out a sigh of relief as he took his weight off his feet. It wasn't long before his eyelids were too heavy to keep open and they drifted shut. No, he couldn't be out like this at night. He had to keep moving, had to keep trying to reach Ollie. He ran his fingers over the cool surface of the walkie-talkie, remembering when Ollie had gotten these things. Ollie and Ben used to use the walkie-talkie and its twin when they would play outside. The two had a habit of straying from their homes when they played hide-and-seek or cops and robbers, using the walkie-talkies to stay in contact and to radio each other about make-believe crimes. Still, they never wandered too far away from each other. It was how Ben knew that Ollie hadn't wandered too far from him this time. Even with everything going on, Ollie was still Ben's partner.

Ben's eyes shot open and he bolted to his feet with a new idea. Cops and robbers, that was it! If anyone could help him, it would be the Lucella Police Department. Ben knew that there was a precinct around here, just a few blocks from where he was. He stuffed the walkie-talkie into his bag. Even if he was out of range now, it was sure to be useful eventually. Lucella was a big island, and Ben would search every inch of it twice if he had to. But with the Infection that turned even the most charming of citizens into violent monsters, Ben was hoping that he would not have to.

Ben ran the rest of the way toward the police station, his heart pounding in his chest and his lungs struggling to pull in as much air as they could. Finally someone who could help him. Ben wasn't a suspicious person by nature, but he slowed his gait as he approached the police station, feeling himself wondering why the lights were off at the precinct when there were still half a dozen cars in the parking lot. He pulled open the doors to the station, stepping into the lobby and flicking a nearby light switch. Fluorescent lights buzzed to life, humming steadily as they flooded the room with a sickly glow. The room was wide and rectangular, and blue strips bearing the insignia of the Lucella Police Department adorned the walls. Ben's shoes, squeaking against the black-and-white tile floor, went silent as he stepped onto the deep red carpet that lined the precinct . . . Ben knew that police stations were supposed to make people feel safe, but he couldn't help but feel ill at ease.

PIGGY:*INFECTED*

"Hello?" Ben cried out, cupping his hands around his mouth and shouting as loudly as he could. "Is anyone here?" There was no response. Ben wandered forward a little, peering around the station. Except for the faint smell of gasoline, the police station looked eerily spotless. The rest of the city was in a state of disrepair—it seemed that keeping up appearances fell down on the list when your city had been besieged by a bizarre virus. Ben couldn't help but wonder when the last time was that someone was here. No one seemed to be in the office, and all the cells used for lockup were empty . . . Then what was that rustling sound? A piece of paper crinkled beneath Ben's foot. Lifting it to his eyes, he read the note hastily scrawled on the side. *To those looking for safety, this is the worst place to look. —TSP.* Well, that was certainly ominous. Ben discarded the piece of paper, wondering what the letters at the end meant. Were they someone's initials? Ben was trying to remember the difference between tea-spoons and tablespoons when his thoughts were interrupted by a high-pitched screeching.

EEEEEE!

Ben jumped, startled by the sound of feedback coming from a pale speaker affixed to the ceiling. The megaphone-looking device blared a single message as clear as day.

"ATTENTION. THERE IS A MONSTER LOOSE IN THE STATION. GET TO THE GARAGE NOW."

Well, that answered several of Ben's questions. He was not alone. Ben looked around for the route to the garage. If there was no one here who could help him, his first priority was getting out of here. There were three paths from the lobby, so one of them had to lead to the garage, right? The growling grunt of an infected Wolf Creature shook him from his decision-making. Like the

26

last one, this infected creature stood at least twice as tall as Ben. Like the last one, this one smelled like leftover waffle batter. And like the last one, this one didn't seem to be in the mood to talk.

The Infected leapt onto the front desk counter and bore down on Ben, who backed away quickly. He had already met one of the Infected earlier this evening, and he wasn't interested in pressing

his luck. When the thing moved toward him, he hesitated before turning to run. The Wolf gave chase, its eyes glowing red just like the infected Pig he had seen outside Ollie's house. Unlike the one outside Ollie's house, though, this one wore a uniform, the Lucella Police Department patch still visible on the shoulder and sleeve. That explained where the fine officers of the Lucella Police Department had gone.

No matter which way Ben ran, the Wolf was there to counter. Taking the middle route, Ben ran into the Sheriff's office, shutting the door behind him. There had to be something in here that could help him. His eyes scanned the room frantically for something, anything he could use to subdue the Infected in the hallways, but the Sheriff's office held absolutely nothing that could help him. Two old computers, a recycling bin, and a handful of potted plants, none of them doing particularly well. The Sheriff's office had two doors, one of which led back into the hallways. Ben used the adjoining door to slip back out into the lobby, much to the chagrin of the infected Wolf. The Infected seemed to have an "out of sight, out of mind" mentality. If their problem wasn't directly in front of them, it didn't seem to exist. In a way, Ben could relate. Unfortunately it seemed that of late, his problems were always directly ahead of him. He would find Ollie. He would find his family. Ben clenched his fists in resolution. It didn't take long for the infected Wolf to catch up with Ben. Luckily for him, there were plenty of places to hide, but it seemed like every time Ben rounded a corner, he was face-to-face with the Infected. Ben held his breath as he peered around another corner separating him from the garage. He had made a wrong turn. Finally cornering Ben, the Wolf Creature raised its arm to strike. Ben recoiled, preparing for a strike that didn't come. Instead, the infected Wolf's growl turned to a gurgle as it hit the ground.

KZZT! The sound of hundreds of volts of electricity echoed throughout the hallway as the Infected writhed on the ground in front of him, its red eyes seemingly more menacing than ever. This was not at all how Ben had thought this night was going to go. Taking a series of shallow breaths, Ben finally managed to pull his eyes away from the infected creature in front of him.

"Well? Are you coming?"

Ben's eyes widened at the first voice he had heard in a long time. He peered around the stunned Wolf to see a tall Dog pointing a Taser, still aimed at the infected creature. He blew on the electrode cartridge, as best as he could with the mouth of a Dog, before twirling the weapon and holstering it. The Dog also wore the uniform of the Lucella Police Department. Ben's jaw dropped.

"*Whoa.* Who are you?"

"Doggy. Officer Doggy. Now come on, that'll only slow 'em down!"

Ben didn't have to be told twice. Gathering what wit he had, he scrambled to his feet, moving past the infected Wolf, who—to Officer Doggy's credit—was no longer moving. In fact, it wasn't doing much of anything . . . but the shot from the Taser was only enough to stun the giant creature. Ben found his footing as he crossed the room to

Officer Doggy, being careful to avoid making any movements that could disturb the Infected. Ben shut the door behind them, then, with Officer Doggy's help, dragged the Sheriff's desk in front of the door, barricading it from the inside. Hopefully that would buy the two some time, something they were in short supply of. Officer Doggy moved through the precinct, leading the way to the garage.

"What is up with those things?" Ben yelled as he tried to keep pace.

"They're not things, kid," Officer Doggy explained as he led Ben down another empty hallway toward the garage. "They're people, just like you and me. Infected by . . . Well, nobody knows. Some kind of virus, an Infection, maybe. I'm guessing you've already figured out that. They're not super friendly. And a hit from one of these will only stun them for about twenty seconds, tops." He held his Taser up, his paws squeezing the device so it made the same unmistakable crackling sound that had just saved

32

Ben's skin a few minutes ago. Somehow, he did not find it comforting.

"Normally this would be the safest place in town, but that was before. Right now we've got to get out of here," Officer Doggy explained. "They have turned the bullpen into a pigpen."

"What?"

"It's, uhh . . . It's a police joke," Officer Doggy said dismissively, his ears moving from front to back.

"Oh. It's, uh . . . very funny," Ben replied, not even sure if he believed himself. He didn't find him-self in the mood for jokes at the moment, even tonally great ones. Officer

Doggy placed his stun gun into its holster again, tail wagging as he peered into the dimly lit garage. "It looks like the coast is clear." Ben mimicked the canine lawman's movements as he, too, peered through the latticed window. Several police cruisers were parked in the garage, but Ben could tell just by looking at them that they were out of commission. The cars that the Lucella Police Department used were new and required constant upkeep. Since the Infection, that just hadn't been possible. Ben's eyes quickly zeroed in on what he knew would be their ticket out of here . . . A faded red two-door that looked older than Ben was. Before the Infection, Ben would have called it a hunk of junk. These days . . . it was still a hunk of junk, but it would have to do. If it meant that they could get out of here and find someone who could help them, then Ben was more than willing to ride in the passenger seat in this lemon of a car. Sure, Officer Doggy made a strong first impression, but he was also the first creature Ben had met recently that didn't immediately try to attack him, which had certainly earned him some brownie points.

"On the count of three. One, two, three!" With Officer Doggy's help, the two forced open the door to the garage—they had both decided it was in their best interests not to try to sneak around the Infected in the bullpen to find a set of keys for this door. The door crunched behind their concerted effort, and Officer Doggy knocked the latch, pulling it off its hinges. The Infected in the police precinct's break room had almost certainly recovered from Officer Doggy's electric assault by now, and try as they might, this wasn't exactly a quiet endeavor. As the door fell off its hinges and clattered to the ground inside the garage, Ben and Officer Doggy quickly made their way to the two-door and hopped into the car, Officer Doggy pulling the keys from the sun visor.

"I thought people only did that in movies," Ben commented.

35

"Well, where do you think we got the idea?" Officer Doggy replied, inserting the keys into the ignition and turning them. Ben had been right about the car being old, but as long as it got them to where they needed to go next, wherever that was, fine. Officer Doggy tried to start the car but was greeted with nothing but the sound of the engine sputtering as it drew in air along with the last dregs of fuel. He revved the engine a few times to no avail. This old rust bucket wouldn't be getting them anywhere without any gas, and if the fuel gauge on the dashboard was any indication, that was exactly the case.

"One working car in the entire neighborhood and it's got no gas?! This feels like it's going to be a problem," Ben said, gritting his teeth in frustration at the turn of events . . .

"No, no problem at all," Officer Doggy replied, his jowls flopping as he shook his head. "There's fuel in the station. Right behind the—"

"Front desk." Ben finished, remembering the faint smell of gasoline he had encountered when he first entered the police station. He would have to make his way back into the police station, through the Sheriff's office, and to the front desk, then bring the gasoline back here and fill up the car, all without alerting the Wolf to his presence. Piece of cake, right? Still, he had to be the one to do it; he needed Officer Doggy to handle the actual driving aspect. Ben let out a deep exhalation, steeling himself for the task at hand.

Stepping out of the car, Ben shut the door behind him, more aware than ever of each sound he made and how any one movement could bring an army of vicious livestock down on him at any moment. Retracing his steps out of the garage, he made his way back into the station. He crept silently through the bullpen, keeping his eyes trained on the Sheriff's office, where the infected officer Wolf slept soundly, just like its counterpart back at Ollie's house. Ben supposed that becoming a mindless monster with an appetite only for destruction probably took a lot out of them. Ben moved as slowly as he could, putting one tender footstep in front of the other until he was close enough to push open the doors to the front lobby. He could see the gasoline now, two bright red cans of it, tapped off with yellow nozzles so that the gas could be inserted directly into a vehicle. That would come in handy, though certainly not as handy as keeping the fuel in the same place as the vehicles. Ben suspected the person in charge of that decision had long since joined the ranks of the Infected. He felt a chill down his spine again, as though he was being watched. Eyes darting to the door, Ben saw a hooded figure outside, hands pressed against the glass. It scared him almost as much as the Wolf, but if he made a sound, the infected Wolf would almost certainly wake up, and that would be that for Ben and likely Officer Doggy. The mysterious figure saw Ben notice it and turned tail, running back down the path. Ben nearly called out after the mystery person. He couldn't give chase; the noise would wake up the Infected sleeping in the Sheriff's office. Not to mention, he couldn't leave Officer Doggy alone like that with no way to escape. Ben climbed over the front desk, grabbing the two jugs of gasoline. They clinked together as Ben hoisted them over the desk. Both of them were a little lighter than Ben would have liked, but anything was better than nothing. It was a small victory, but even those were in short supply these days.

Ben looked back at the Sheriff's empty office as he hefted the gasoline onto his shoulders. Empty? Ben did a double take. His eyes were not deceiving him—the Wolf was awake. It lumbered at him from across the room, its glowing red eye trained on Ben's delicious noggin. Or maybe it wanted the gasoline. The Infected didn't seem to be keen on making their motives clear. So far they seemed to issue a lot of confusing grunts and then attack with large melee weapons. Ben threw one of the gasoline containers at the advancing Wolf. Ben wasn't sure what effect he had expected the canister to have, but it had none. It didn't seem to irritate the creature. In fact, Ben wouldn't be surprised to learn that it didn't even register. The thing advanced as Ben made his way around the reception desk with the sole remaining jug of gasoline, the fuel inside sloshing loudly as Ben ran away from the Infected.

Moving through the Sheriff's office, Ben knocked over anything he could find to impede the Wolf's progress. Potted plants, chairs, and the Sheriff's recycling bin all fell to the wayside as Ben tried to put anything that he could between himself and the Infected. Again, the creature was hardly bothered, cutting through anything in its path like it was nothing. Ben pushed through the garage door,

Officer Doggy honking the car's horn impatiently. The sound echoed throughout the empty garage, only serving to draw the Wolf's attention.

Ben's hands trembled with nerves and adrenaline as he unscrewed the gas cap on the car and held the gas jug between his thighs, inserting the nozzle into the fuel tank of the car. He lifted the jug, pouring as much of the gasoline down into the tank as he could, jostling the canister to shake every possible drop out of it. He knew that he would reach a point of diminishing returns, and quickly, but when the city you had grown up in was overrun by an army of Infected, every drop counted. The canister depleted, Ben shouted for Officer Doggy to start the engine, and just in time, too. The infected Wolf was at the garage door, and he looked ready to give chase. For a moment, Ben almost felt bad. The creature still had on its Lucella Police Department uniform. It had had some sort of life before all . . . this. Then again, so had Ben. Ben tossed the empty gasoline jug into a nearby trash can as he slid into the passenger seat of the car and slammed the door, the noise enraging the Wolf.

Officer Doggy stuck the keys back into the ignition, turning them as the car tried its best to sputter to life. Its best wasn't good enough, and Ben could see the infected Wolf was advancing on them in the rearview mirror. Officer Doggy continued trying to start the car, the Wolf looming ever larger in the car's headlights, reflected against the garage doors. The Infected stumbled down the stairs, its labored breathing making Ben aware of the fact that he was holding his own breath and had been for several seconds. The thing reached out, its hand nearly on the latch for the side door, when the engine sprang into action. Turning over, the engine rattled, shook, and roared to life. Ben was no automotive expert. He didn't know what sounds cars were supposed to make, but he definitely knew which sounds they weren't, and this car was making about a half dozen of those. But as long as it got them away from being wolfed, Ben didn't much care.

The garage door, which Officer Doggy had activated using a remote on the car's dashboard, opened slowly, giving them just enough clearance to get through once the car started, the garage door scraping gently on the roof of the car. Officer Doggy shifted the vehicle out of park and into drive, tearing away from the police department and leaving the Wolf quite literally in their dust, a cloud of black soot erupting from somewhere under the car's hood as they started to accelerate. As they pulled away from the station and shot down the street, Officer Doggy honked the car's horn in raucous celebration. Even Ben, tired as he was, couldn't help but make a small smile.

The two drove without speaking for a while. They were both trying to catch their breath, both trying to conserve energy, and both trying to process

what they had seen this evening. But this quiet wasn't like the quiet on the street or in the police station. It felt relaxing, almost safe. Ben even drifted in and out of sleep for a few moments, then jerked back awake by every red light that reminded him of the haunting eyes of the Infected, or a stop sign that looked in the shadows like an eight-foot-tall Pig. There was something to be said for Officer Doggy obeying the rules of the road, even when they were the only car around. The headlights illuminated a few feet in front of the car, but for Ben, it wasn't nearly enough.

"You're lucky I showed up on my day off, kid," Officer Doggy said, breaking the silence and interrupting Ben's haunting thoughts. He pulled a bottle from the backseat and popped it open, the rainbow-colored liquid inside the bottle sloshing around as they drove down the bumpy street. Officer Doggy took a sip and offered it to Ben, who declined.

"You're lucky I remembered where that gasoline was," Ben groggily replied. Their escape had been a team effort, and if they had not pulled it together, it might not have even been a successful one.

"Touché, kid. Man, we really need to find out what's going on." Doggy kept his paws on the steering wheel, not taking his eyes off the road.

The car continued to sputter and shake. What had seemed to rock him to sleep just a few moments ago now threatened to shake him like salad dressing.

"I know," replied Ben, "I've started to see these things all over the place." Ben couldn't remember exactly when the Infection had started sweeping across the island, but there was no denying that there had been an uptick in cases over the last few weeks. It was another reason that he hoped his family had made it into one of the encampments that had been popping up all over the island.

"We have to find out what is causing this. Luckily I haven't lost any of my past detective skills," boasted Officer Doggy, his ears stiffening on top of his head. "You got any skills of your own?"

Ben thought about it. It wasn't a question that he had ever been asked before. He was smart, he thought, but no genius. He could keep pace with his friends when they played sports, but he was certainly no athlete. He had a few hobbies but couldn't think of anything he could do that would qualify as a skill. In the movie where the jewel thief comes out of retirement for one last job and phones his most skilled associates, Ben was not waiting by the phone.

After a moment, Ben answered, "I hope so. I think I could use them more now than ever before."

"I hope so, too," Officer Doggy said, taking almost as long to reply. "I really do. So, you got a name, kid?"

"It's, uhh . . . Ben. Just Ben. And why are we slowing down?"

Officer Doggy cocked a brow, wondering the same thing. The veteran of the force's eyes flitted across the dashboard, eventually finding the fuel gauge. "Umm . . . how much gasoline did you put in the car?" Officer Doggy asked, trying to keep panic from beginning to rise in his voice.

"I don't know," Ben replied. "However much was left. I wasn't exactly at the pump." Ben already knew the problem. However much gas they had in the car, it was enough to get them away from the police station but not nearly enough to get them out of town.

The car rolled to a halt, the inertia sending the occupants gently rocking. Every one of Officer Doggy's attempts to get it started again only seemed to make the problem worse, until the car was almost literally screaming in protest. "I'll get out and see if there's anything I can do," Officer Doggy said, stepping out of the car. Ben locked his door, not knowing what good it would do for anything but his peace of mind. He had encountered two of the Infected tonight, and neither of them had been big on door etiquette. With his face pressed against the cool window, he watched as Officer Doggy stepped into the crisp, dark night and lifted up the hood of the old car. The machine sputtered and hissed, but it seemed as if there was nothing that Officer Doggy could do to get it to start again. Ben rolled down his window, hoping the cool air would help him collect his thoughts. It worked for a moment. The wind blew through his hair, the fresh air almost refreshing. He closed his eyes and took in deep breaths, soon gulping down lungfuls of oxygen. He was so happy to be away from the infected Wolf back at the police station, he didn't even mind the smells in the air. The gasoline from the fuel tank, the acrid cloud of black smoke hanging in the air over the car's engine, and . . . something else. *Oh no.*

"Officer Doggy. Get back . . . in the car . . . !" Ben urgently whispered through gritted teeth, but it was too late. Out of the darkness, he saw five of the Infected approach, surrounding the car from every angle. Their eyes glowed in the darkness, and their wrinkled clothes and distinctive grunts and groans told Ben that they were all

Infected, even if their smell hadn't conveyed that very message. One of them, a Pig, wore a tattered purple dress. It was clear that it had at one time been a nice garment, though it could use a good wash these days. From the sight of the splintered piece of wood in her hand, laundry was not high on the infected Pig's priority list. A Cat, almost as tall as Ben, wore a dirty set of coveralls and a matching cap, though whether the dirt had appeared before or after the Infection was anyone's guess. A third that Ben could see from his vantage point inside the vehicle appeared to be a Lamb, her wool knotted with dirt and caked with mud. In her hand, she wielded a blunt gardening tool.

Ben wondered for a moment how they'd been found, before the car sputtered and coughed as if to answer his question. If the Infected were drawn to sound, this car was practically a neon arrow pointing to Ben and Officer Doggy. Bathed in the headlights of the stalled car, Ben couldn't decide if their assailants were more or less frightening in the light. Their skin was waxy and pale, and their eyes glowed creepily, reflecting the light. The five infected creatures stood around the car, almost as if they were each waiting for another to make the first move. One of the Infected even still wore a pair of reading glasses. It would be haunting and sad, if they weren't each carrying a wooden club or a metal pipe and advancing so menacingly on Ben and Officer Doggy.

Officer Doggy scrambled onto the hood of the car and then the roof, putting as much distance between him and the clammy monsters as he could. Ben had never seen so many of the Infected gather in one place. They had probably heard the clunker coming for miles, and the duo running out of gas had provided an opportunity that they couldn't resist. Ben turned the crank to roll up his window quickly, already losing control of the breaths he had just worked so hard for. "Stay close to me while I think of a plan!" Officer Doggy shouted through the window to Ben, as if Ben had much of a choice. His alternative was to get out of the car and try to make friends, and Ben was inclined to find Ollie before he started entertaining other offers of friendship. Officer Doggy pulled out his stun gun and fired a single Taser round at one of the Infected. The shot landed true, striking the infected Wolf, but Ben knew that was a temporary solution. In twenty seconds, that same Wolf would be up and moving around again.

"Okay! So what's the plan?" Ben asked, willing the window to close faster as one of the Infected began to reach in. The Infected were closing in on all sides, Ben was beginning to feel a little bit claustrophobic, and the numbers were not on their side.

"Run!" Officer Doggy shouted, leaping over one of the Infected's heads and making a break toward the nearest building. Half the infected creatures broke off to chase him, the dull-minded creatures seemingly always in the mood to give chase. That was the best-laid plan of one of Lucella's finest? Ben was really reconsidering whether or not he was going to make it out of this unscathed. The Infected on the other side of the car pressed their faces against the closed car window like Ben was a particularly interesting fish in a tank. Their breath fogged the window; their eyes were blank and red and cold. If this was what it was like to fall to the Infected, he hoped fervently that Ollie hadn't suffered the same fate. Ollie. He still had to find his friend. If it was his fate to be torn apart by a monster Cow, then fate could wait. With reckless abandon, Ben threw his door open and ran after Officer Doggy.

Officer Doggy held the door of the nearest building open for Ben. The Infected who had remained behind were now also in pursuit, five of the

Infected chasing Ben and Officer Doggy. A side effect of the sickness seemed to slow down some of the Infected; it wasn't terribly difficult for Ben to overtake them and catch up with Officer Doggy. Without the element of surprise, most of the Infected were your average, everyday, eight-foot-tall monster people . . . Rushing past Officer Doggy, Ben pulled Doggy into the building, helping him shut the door on the quintet of Infected.

"We have to find a way to get out of here, Officer Doggy. There's way too many of them," Ben said, wiping sweat from his brow. Catching his breath had recently become a waste of time.

"I know," Officer Doggy agreed, his nose twitching as he sniffed the air around them. "Look, we're close to a campsite. We can get some rest, regroup, and think about what our next move is." Ben agreed silently, swallowing dryly as they made their way through the building. The campgrounds on the edge of town weren't a bad idea.

The Infected didn't seem to have spread that far yet, and Ben couldn't remember the last time he had gotten a good night's sleep. Officer Doggy limped ahead. Some day off he was having. Now that he wasn't running for his life, Ben recognized this place as the old Lucella Gallery. Caution tape adorned the doorway. *Maybe they're remodeling*, Ben thought optimistically. More likely, there was something more sinister happening. One of the Infected tried to force its way into the gallery. It was Ben's fault; he had gotten lazy and hadn't barricaded the door behind them. Ben ran to the door, looking around for some piece of modern art he could move in front of the door. They all looked the same to him, but maybe that was the point? Maybe the true art was— Another loud thud sounded against the door, making Ben's decision seem trivial. Ben pushed a statue in front of the door, the Infected on the other side of the door vocally displeased. Another thud, but this time not against the door, against the . . . floor?

Did he dare look outside and see what had happened?

He waited another few moments before his curiosity got the better of him and then Ben pulled the door ajar, just a crack. It was surprisingly easy— maybe his barricade wouldn't have been as effective as he hoped. At the foot of the door lay one of the infected creatures, alive but clearly out of it. Through the slit in the doorway, Ben could make out shapes. A tiny frame, a flared hood . . . the hooded figure from the police station! Ben tried to open the door farther to get a better look but found it blocked by the statue. The hooded figure whacked the infected Lamb, and the creature went down with a deranged bleat.

"Hey!" Ben called out, trying to get the hooded figure's attention. Then again, he didn't quite know what he would say—*Who are you? Thank you?*—but it didn't matter. Seemingly spooked by Ben's outburst, the hooded figure disappeared.

Ben groaned in frustration, then shut the door quickly. He wasn't sure how much time these creatures would stay down, but it never seemed to be too long.

There were still some of the creatures whose whereabouts Ben had not accounted for. He was moving the statue back against the door when he saw a note tacked to the base. He pulled it off slowly, the handwriting instantly recognizable. He had seen one almost exactly like it back at the police station. *TSP.* Maybe those were the initials of the mysterious hooded figure? Ben was deep in thought, when something reached out, gripping his shoulder. Ben nearly jumped out of his skin, frantically searching for the nearest blunt object. Officer Doggy threw up his paws, expressing his innocence. "Hey, why so high-strung?" Officer Doggy asked, stepping into the light.

"Oh, you know . . . just normal kid stuff," Ben replied dryly, placing his hand over his heart.

"Oh. Really?"

"No, it's definitely the crazy virus that's trans-forming everyone on the island into a monster, Officer Doggy."

"Ah. Who were you shouting at?" the patrolman asked quietly, but it was too late, and too much to explain. How did you casually drop that you thought you were being stalked by a hooded mon-ster slayer into casual conversation? Without proof, it would sound like Ben was losing his mind.

"Just . . . don't worry about it. Let's get out of here." Officer Doggy and Ben worked together, dragging a large onyx statue of a Pig in front of the gallery door. Ben was sure the owners wouldn't mind—mostly because like most of the city of Lucella, Ben couldn't tell when the last time was that someone had been here. The paintings that lined the halls—beautiful as they were—were all askew, and everything in the building was coated in a fine layer of dust. This was not the well-maintained and refined Lucella Art Gallery Ben had been to so many times as a child. Ben straightened a portrait as the two of them walked down the hallway.

Officer Doggy let out a deep breath, his ears twitching beneath his cap.

"Man, they just don't stop coming for us, do they?" He seemed to almost chuckle with the realization. Ben had endured a long night—he couldn't imagine what Officer Doggy had seen at the police station before Ben got there. "It's nothing we can't handle. Good ol' Officer Doggy has made crazier arrests."

Ben's ears perked up. "You have? Crazier than those things? They're a bunch of monsters, and all they do is attack us." Officer Doggy stopped, and Ben straightened another portrait of a Pig in a frame.

"Look, kid. You're a good person. Even in desperate times, you hold on to your morals. It's the people like you who succeed. As long as you stay true to who you are, you'll get to where you need to be." He patted Ben's shoulder and walked ahead, the light from his flashlight illuminating the way.

Ben stayed back, letting Officer Doggy's words wash over him. But Doggy was right. Ben couldn't let this situation make him lose sight of who he was, or why he was here. He was going to find his friend, and he was going to get him back home safely. That was why he had started out on this journey, and he wasn't going home until he'd completed it. *Hold on, Ollie, wherever you are. I'm coming for you.* He was interrupted from his thoughts by a howling yelp. Officer Doggy! Ben heard the commotion in the next room and ran toward it, screaming as he found Officer Doggy on the floor, the policeman reaching for his Taser. Two of the infected creatures from the car stood over him, now distracted by Ben's arrival.

"Ben!" Officer Doggy yelled, gesturing pointedly toward the stun gun, which had fallen from his grasp. Ben fumbled for the device, pointing it and successfully stunning one of the large creatures. He aimed it at the second, this time getting nothing more than an unsatisfactory click. It was out of cartridges. Ben grabbed Officer Doggy by the paw, hauling him to his feet. Running past the stunned Pig Creature, Ben and Officer Doggy found their way blocked by the other creature. Red eye flaring, the Cat raised its arm, swiping at Ben and Officer Doggy. Ben managed to dodge, pulling open the door behind it. The two scurried away from the Cat, even as the Pig began to stir, shaking off the effects of the Taser.

Closing the door behind them and blocking it with a pair of ornate stanchions, Officer Doggy and Ben made their way down the gallery stairs, past the Mid-Century art exhibit, and down through the Ancient Times display. Officer Doggy leaned against Ben, gathering his strength as he examined his body where the Pig had swiped him.

"Are you all right, Officer?" Ben asked, knowing that it didn't look good. Even when there wasn't an Infection going around, getting attacked in a museum by creatures you didn't know wasn't a vaunted line of action . . .

"Of course, kid. It's only a flesh wound. Just . . . give me a minute." Ben held on to Officer Doggy, but it didn't feel like they had a minute to spare, and flesh wounds were among the worst kinds of wounds to get, certainly top ten. Ben could hear the band of infected creatures making their way down the stairs, could smell the odor of burnt hair soaked in old milk. As soon as Officer Doggy gave him the word, he hoisted the police officer to his feet and pushed open the back door.

The sun was finally coming up, and Ben didn't think he had ever seen anything as beautiful as this sunrise. Officer Doggy took point, doing his shaky best to lead them through the forest as the sun rose over the island. The air was crisper out here, each breath felt like a lungful of hope, and it was a nice change of pace. Maybe it was because he knew that this was the closest to safety he had been since he had last seen his family. For the last several hours, he had been dealing with a barrage of smells—everything from gasoline to Infected—but for the first time he could remember in a long time, he could actually breathe.

"This your safe space, Officer Doggy?" Ben asked, balling his jacket into a makeshift pillow as he collapsed onto a nearby log.

"My family and I used to come out here when we wanted to get away from it all," Doggy answered. "I've never wanted to get away so badly in my life." He groaned as the two settled down at an abandoned campsite.

"Are you okay, Officer Doggy? If one of those things back there—"

"I'm fine!" Officer Doggy snapped back, probably a bit more aggressively than he meant. "I'm fine. I just need to get a little rest. Let's get some sleep. We can think of what to do next in the morning. Even a detective of my caliber can't solve the Mystery of the Missing Forty Winks!"

"Doggy? I think those things . . . I think they were our friends. I think they used to be . . . like us," Ben said out loud for the first time, his voice quivering with uncertainty.

"Get some sleep, kid," Officer Doggy said, repeating himself. He didn't seem to want to talk about it, and Ben wouldn't push him. The Wolf at police headquarters might have been his friend. The Infected outside Ollie's house might have been . . . Suddenly Ben understood why Officer Doggy didn't want to talk about it.

"Sounds like a plan," Ben agreed. He wasn't used to certain creature comforts, but this was certainly roughing it. Ten hours ago, he had been looking for his best friend. Now he was in the middle of the forest, hiding from an island of infected people with a police officer while being hunted by a mysterious figure in a hood . . . Ben didn't even have time to comment on the weirdness of it all; he was asleep as soon as his head hit his pillow.

Ben didn't know how much time had passed since he woke up. The fire Officer Doggy had crafted out of a few dry branches from the forest was now dying down, its embers casting dancing shadows on the nearby trees. Smoke spiraled lazily into the air, the few stars visible above the island twinkling down on Ben. It seemed as if even the island-wide fog had no jurisdiction over the forests of Lucella. He stood and stretched, his joints

aligning into place the way they could only after sleeping for far too long on a fallen tree in the middle of the forest. He looked around for Officer Doggy, but the policeman was nowhere to be seen. For a moment, he thought that his companion might have stepped away to gather more firewood, but as he waited near the dying fire, the far more likely possibility began to creep into Ben's mind. He had seen the infected Pig swipe at Officer Doggy back at the gallery. Either Officer Doggy had left in the middle of the night to get help, or he had left because he knew he was becoming one of those things and he wanted to spare Ben the same fate. Either way, Ben was alone again, just as he had been at the beginning of last night. It was becoming a familiar feeling.

Ben sat back down on a log near the campsite, watching the fire die out slowly as the sun rose again. So far, this place had been the safest haven he had come across, even safer than the police station. He had no leads on Ollie's whereabouts, no car to drive anywhere, and now no partner. He decided to wait it out; maybe Officer Doggy would return. But the longer Ben stayed at the campsite, the more he was proven correct on what he had known all along. Officer Doggy would not be coming back. Hours passed, turning into days, turning into weeks, or maybe it just felt that way. All Ben did was eat, sleep, and watch for the Infected, though even that was proving to be a fruitless endeavor. He hadn't seen one since that night at the gallery. Maybe Doggy had been right about this place—maybe it was the one place on the island that was truly safe from the Infection. At least during the day.

Ben had the same dream every night. The first few times, he had thought it was a nightmare; now it was as much a part of his routine as brushing his teeth. Every night, Ben would fall asleep and dream that he was out looking for Ollie. Ben would call his name, the sound echoing across the street until Ollie opened his front door, a familiar smile plastered across his face. Ollie would start laughing and Ben would cross the street to his friend, but the closer Ben got to Ollie, the farther away he seemed. Ben tried to move faster, but it was like running through quicksand. Every night, by the time he finally got to Ollie's front porch, it was too late. Ollie's skin had gone pale, his eyes glowing red. And every night, that's when Ben would wake.

KRSSH!

Ben awoke with a start, bolting upright and wiping sweat from his brow. He was less than fond of that dream, but these days, it was the only way he got to see his missing friend. Ben shook his head as if that would help to clear it, moving toward his backpack and riffling through it, looking for a bottle of water. He found it quickly, unscrewed the cap, and downed half the bottle in a frenzy of thirst. Being the only person you knew was thirsty work.

KRSSH!

Ben raised a brow, trying to discern the source of the strange sound. He had been alone for so long that if someone were trying to get the jump on him, they would have to be a whole lot quieter than whatever that was. The sound came through again, this time followed by a voice.

"H-hello?"

Ben remembered as soon as he heard the voice. He had taken Ollie's walkie-talkie from his house— someone must be trying to get in contact with him. He tore open the backpack's various compartments and pouches, desperately trying to remember where in the backpack he had tucked away the walkie-talkie. "Hello?" In frustration, Ben turned the bag upside down and began to shake it, the walkie-talkie tumbling out and falling with a dull thud against the damp forest floor. Ben practically leapt on it, holding the transmission button.

"Hello? Hello, Ollie?!" Ben called frantically into the cheap plastic two-way. Ben released the transmission button, waiting for a response from the other side. The line went silent, even the static cutting out. Ben could hear his heart pounding in his ears. All this time and he finally might get to see his best friend.

"Hello? Ollie!" Ben repeated, hoping that his friend on the other end was simply too choked up with emotion to respond to his words. Ben sat against a tree, his hands falling to his side as the line went dead once more. But then . . . a crackle.

"I don't know an Ollie"—**KRRSH!**—"I'm sorry!"

Ben's heart sank for what must have been the fiftieth time in recent memory. He took his hand off the transmission button, making sure that no one caught the sob in his throat. Holding the walkie-talkie back to his mouth, he spoke into it calmly and matter-of-factly.

"Sorry, sir. I'm looking for someone," Ben replied, his mouth going dry. He realized that this was the first person he had spoken to since Officer Doggy. He silently hoped that they would not suffer the same fate.

"Don't be sorry, dear boy! I'm looking for someone, too!" came the voice on the other end.

"You . . . are?" asked Ben, incredulous. Of course with everything going on, there would be others like Ben, other people searching for loved ones.

"We must have gotten our frequencies crossed; it happens all the time," the voice on the other end of the line said, as though he were discussing the weather. Sure enough, when Ben looked down at the walkie-talkie, it was set to channel 2, when Ollie and Ben had always used channel 3 to communicate with each other. Was that what had gone wrong? Had he been sending out distress calls and location scouts to the wrong walkie-talkie for what amounted to most of his journey? He thought back to what Officer Doggy had said about skills.

"Oh. Well, uhh . . . Thanks for the heads-up. I hope you find who you're looking for."

Ben was ready to end the call, but a hurried "Wait, wait, wait!" came through the walkie-talkie's speaker. Ben placed the two-way back to his ear. "You have to help me! I need you to rescue my friend from the—" **KRRSH!**

Ben held down the transmission button, just to make sure that he had heard the voice correctly. "I'm sorry, sir. You want me to rescue your friend from where?"

"The school, young man! The school!" Ben stifled his reaction. Even if the Lucella School District wasn't a hike from his location, Ben couldn't think of a place he would least like to be in this situation. The school was a poorly lit building with way too many rooms for the Infected to hide in. So far he had been attacked by one of those things in just about every building he had entered. He would take his chances in nature. Ben was about to tell the mysterious voice on the other end that he was on his own when another garbled transmission came through on the walkie-talkie. "Please." **KRSSH!** "She's all I have left."

Ben wasn't sure if it was the man's tone or his words that got to him, but he knew how he felt. To be moving through this world without the people and things that gave you joy wasn't moving through this world at all. If this Infection was going to teach him any lesson, it's that life is only worth living when people were living for one another. Ben held down the transmission button.

"I'll . . . I'm going to see what I can do," Ben said, already regretting committing to this journey. It was completely out of his way, and if he didn't know how long it had been since he had last been into town, there was no way to know just how bad the Infection had gotten. Had everyone contracted the sickness by now? Would Ben even be able to make it into the city without being spotted or attacked?

"Oh, thank you, young man! Thank you, thank you, thank you!" Maybe it was the fact that Ben hadn't spoken to anyone else in weeks, but the gratitude in the stranger's voice made Ben well up. Of course he was going to try to help. It was what he would have wanted someone else to do for him.

Packing up his few belongings—some food, Ollie's walkie-talkie, and Officer Doggy's Taser—and stowing them away for safekeeping, he began the trip back into town. By the time he reached the city limits, it was dark again. He debated waiting until morning to try to reach the school, but if things were as bad as Ben assumed they were, his new friend's friend might not make it until morning. Officer Doggy hadn't. Ben tried the front door of the school building and was surprised to find it already open. He had been prepared to sneak around, maybe find a missing key or a few exposed gears somewhere, and jimmy his way into the school. This seemed a lot simpler. Ben could tell immediately that he was in territory that had been occupied by the Infected. If not because of the smell of wet hair or the sound of heavy breathing as soon as Ben opened the door, then because of the mess.

The school looked almost exactly the way that Ben remembered it from when he had taken classes here, but the entire building was in disarray. Papers were strewn on the floor between classrooms, desks were ajar and askew, and the entire building seemed to be coated in the kind of dust that you only find at construction sites. The front door shut lightly behind him. Ben was basically an expert at shutting doors silently now. He crept inside, the halls still illuminated by a series of overhead lights that gave the entire building a garish shine. Spray-painted across a set of lockers was DO NOT OPEN, MONSTER INSIDE. —TSP. Ben thought it a good idea to take TSP at their word.

Ben tiptoed through the school, checking each classroom for anyone who might be friends with the voice on the other end of his walkie-talkie, but his search was proving fruitless. Ben noticed one of the infected creatures sleeping in the science lab, flat on its back across one of the lab tables, drool pooling at the corner of its mouth. At least the Infected hadn't changed while Ben had been away. He passed another in the math classroom, this one standing asleep against a blackboard. Backing gingerly away, Ben pulled open another door. This room was different.

Instead of chalkboards and desks, this room had only tables and chairs. The cafeteria. Ben made a beeline for the back, opening the fridge and stuffing his face with anything he could find. Having spent the last several weeks living in the woods, he wasn't as picky with his culinary choices as he might otherwise have been.

The food that Ben helped himself to had created a solid mass in his stomach, a stomach not at all used to being full. Cracking open a bottle of off-brand juice, Ben poured the artificial flavors down his throat, letting out a satisfied sigh as he felt the liquid hit his stomach. Maybe this rescue mission wasn't the worst idea. Then again, he would actually have to finish the "rescue" part for it to count. He had spent the last few weeks judging the infected creatures for only giving in to their base impulses to feed and fight, but if he looked at himself right now, he was doing the same thing. He emptied the contents of the fridge into his backpack. If he was this hungry, he couldn't imagine what state his potential rescue would be in when he found her.

Ben grabbed the backpack, silently thanking Officer Doggy for leaving it with him, wherever he was. Now all he had to do was find Walkie-Talkie's forgotten friend. Ben let the refrigerator door shut as he zipped his backpack shut. The refrigerator door clattered against the now-empty shelves, the sound echoing throughout the empty building. Ben craned his neck out of the cafeteria to see if the Infected creature in the science lab was still asleep, but he knew the answer already. He couldn't hear the characteristic snoring; he knew what that meant. The Infected were awake.

His suspicions were confirmed when he saw one of the Infected at the end of the hall. This was the one from the math classroom, its ripped orange shirt still marked with chalk dust from the black-board. Ben froze in his tracks. Every fiber of his being told him to turn around and run, but that would only draw more attention. Plus, there was still the science-lab Infected left unaccounted for. Ben continued to stand still, frozen in time to any Infected or person who might come across him. With nothing to see, nothing to do, and nothing to chase, the Infected continued stiffly up the stairs, waiting for its next opportunity to attack. It wouldn't have one, if Ben had anything to say about it. As the Infected passed, Ben went to work. He examined the hammer he pulled out of Officer Doggy's bag with an eye of admiration. It was just one of the tools Ben had used to survive in the forest. It had been dulled from use, but it would serve its purpose.

Ben had been using it to build, but hammers could take things apart just as easily as they could assemble them. Making sure that the Infected had returned to its home base of the math classroom, Ben went to work, pulling nails out of the floorboards and putting them into his bag. Once again,

he thought back to Officer Doggy and their talk
about skills. The good thing about skills was that
it was never too late to learn new ones. The job
didn't take long, and it would have been even
quicker if Ben hadn't been so afraid to make noise.
But now that was the goal. Ben pulled the hammer
out of the floorboard with a dull **thwack!**
Even this small amount of noise was enough to
lure the Infected back, but this time Ben was
ready. The Infected approached him as they all
did, slowly—almost lumbering toward him, and
raising whatever weapon they had. This particular
Infected carried with it a jagged yardstick. For a
moment, Ben wondered who this had been before
it was infected. But only for a moment. Ben's trap
worked, and as the Infected took another halted,
lurching step toward Ben, it tumbled through the
floor, now loosened up by Ben's handiwork. Ben
peered through the floor at the Infected, who had
landed, stunned.

Ben's celebration was cut short, however, when he heard a scream from the lower level. It wasn't like the squeals of the infected creatures, all guttural and grunting. No, this was a scream of terror, a scream that sent shivers down his spine—a sensation he should be used to at this point. Running down the stairs, he leapt over the unconscious Infected, following the sound of the screaming. The sound led him down a hallway, just past where the Infected had fallen through the floor. This must be Ben's mysterious friend's mysterious friend, Ben reasoned. No one understood just how scary these things could be, but if his new companion couldn't curtail her understandable urge to scream, they would have more of the creatures on their tails than they could handle. Ben was reminded of the group of infected creatures outside the art gallery, attracted at first to the car's honking horn, and later to the sputtering sounds the vehicle made as it ran out of fuel.

Ben quickly pulled the door down, now using his trusty hammer to pull the hinges off the door. It was a small closet, likely used for mops and brooms when this place was a school, but now it was home to the Infected's latest victim. She was about Ben's height, huddled in the corner among the boxes of old sponges and packs of chalk. Yet another scream hitched in her throat as Ben tore the door off, before she realized that Ben was not one of *them*. The girl had light brown skin, and she wore a small, cyan-tinted white dress. Two short ears stood atop her head, accentuated by the fact that she would twitch her head every few seconds. Her dark eyes were offset by glowing white pupils, and her nose was light pink, settled plainly between her small, dark red cheeks. She took in another sharp inhalation of breath, Ben quickly interrupting what he assumed to be the prelude to another scream.

"Hi. Long story, but I'm here to help get you out of here," Ben explained quietly. There was still at least one of the infected creatures left, and Ben wasn't sure if he had finished off the one who had fallen into his trap.

The captive nodded emphatically, tiny ears jostling slightly forward as she did. "Sally," she said, introducing herself.

"Nice to meet you," Ben said, already looking for a way out of the school. If Ben had learned anything in the last few weeks, it was the importance of an escape route. "My name is Ben. Friend of yours sent me here to rescue you," Ben explained as he tucked his hammer back into his backpack. The food he had stuffed into the bag earlier rose to the surface as he dug around for a place to put the hammer.

"Are you hungry?" Ben offered, his bag currently boasting enough ill-gotten gains to feed them both for at least the time it would take them to get back to the safe zone in the forest. Sally's nose twitched, her ears swiveling forward on top of her head as

Ben showed her his stash. Slowly she reached for two acorns, the first of the two disappearing into her mouth. As she spoke, brown acorn crumbs spilled out of her mouth and down the front of her white dress.

"Sorry. Sweet tooth," Sally apologized, but Ben chuckled. He understood. If only someone had been there with a bag of sweets when he first woke up inside Ollie's house all that time ago. Sally took a swig from the stoppered glass vial in Officer Doggy's bag, drinking down some of the rainbow-colored liquid inside before wiping her mouth with the back of her hand. "Sorry, but it has just been me and my bow here for days! We were hiding out in the school gym until those . . . things came in and took over the school."

Ben zipped his bag, throwing it back over his shoulder. The walkie-talkie voice hadn't said anything about a second rescue, and Ben and Sally were skating on thin ice as it was. There was still one of the infected creatures unaccounted for, and as ingenious as his trap was, there was no telling how long the Infected would be out of commission. Ben let out a sigh. He had come this far—he wasn't going to leave anyone behind.

"Do you know where your beau is now?"

Sally raised a furrowed brow. "My bow? Well, its right here, isn't it?" Sally turned, reaching back into the closet to pull out a piece of small wooden machinery—a crossbow.

"Your *bow*," Ben repeated as the realization dawned on him. "Great! Let's go." Ben extended his hand, helping Sally to her feet. She brushed dust and acorn crumbs from her dress onto the floor, and together, they exited the storage closet. The infected creature whom Ben had laid a trap for upstairs still lay on the floor outside the room, both the wind and consciousness knocked out of it for the time being. They stepped cautiously over the Pig Creature's sleeping body. Even if Ben was proud of how his trap had worked out, he knew better than anyone that it didn't take much noise at all to wake one of these creatures up and alert them to your presence. In the hallway, Ben screwed his eyes shut tightly, trying to remember the way he had planned to get out of the school. He would just have to retrace his steps.

"Uhh . . . Ben?" Sally tapped Ben's shoulder nervously, several times.

"Not now, Sally. I'm trying to find us a way out of here," Ben said, opening his eyes. This set of lockers looked familiar. Logic dictated that if he followed landmarks, anything that looked like he had already seen it, eventually they would reach the exit.

"Why don't you just ask them?" Ben had to look to see what she was talking about. Were there more survivors here in the school? His gaze followed Sally's, eyes finally landing where her finger was pointing before going wide.

The science lab Infected was lumbering toward them, woken from its beauty sleep, and not a moment too soon. A pack of other Infected joined it, their glowing red eyes shining ominously against the backdrop of the classrooms that they had come from. Ben put himself between Sally and the new infected creatures. He drew his hammer from Officer Doggy's backpack. He wished that Officer Doggy had left him a bigger hammer, but it was better than nothing. Ben had seen the alternative, and he was not a fan.

"Stay behind me. Don't make a move. And when I say so, we need to run." Ben waited for Sally's response, anything to acknowledge that she had heard him and that they were on the same page. Instead, he was greeted by a soft crunching sound. Ignoring his instincts to keep his eyes trained on the Infected, Ben turned to look at Sally. Sally nodded at Ben as she crunched quickly on the other acorn she had taken from Officer Doggy's backpack. Ben's eyes went wide at her timing— the thought of possibly being eaten didn't do much to stir Ben's appetite, but to each their own. Sally continued to gnaw on the acorn until she had chewed it down into into a cone shape, making it sharper at the end. She twisted the newly made arrowhead onto the end of a stick and fitted it to her bow, raising the contraption to the level of her eye. She screwed up her face in concentration, closed one eye, and fired.

The arrow flew true, launching itself out of Sally's bow with impressive force. The acorn whistled through the air, striking the Infected from the science classroom right between its glowing red eyes. The creature wobbled on its feet, stunned by the force of the airborne missile. Ben couldn't help but let out an incredulous cheer. Another infected creature from another classroom reacted to the sound, advancing on Ben and Sally.

"I can't believe that worked!" Ben admitted as he and Sally backed away from the Infected. The monstrous thing continued to move toward them until they could go no farther, their backs pressed against a row of purple lockers.

"I guess this is it for us," Sally bemoaned. "If only I hadn't eaten our ammo!"

The creature swiped at them, missing as Ben pushed Sally out of the way. Still, the creature caught her arm with its claws, and she let out a bellow of pain.

"This way!" Ben yelled, running toward the conference room, holding off an infected Tiger with his hammer. Sally took off after him, moving as quickly as she could while gripping her arm. The infected creatures followed Ben and Sally down the hall as Ben managed to force the door open, the first of the Infected having recovered from the stunning effect that Sally's bow had. The Infected made their way into the conference room, lumbering about the office space looking for their prey.

With careful steps, Ben and Sally snuck out the other side of the conference room, slamming the door shut behind them and placing Ben's hammer through the latch, effectively trapping the Infected in the conference room. Ben and Sally cheered for themselves, elated in their own ingenuity. It wouldn't last, but it was clever enough to buy the duo time to get out of the school. Ben collapsed to his knees, exhausted. Pulling Ollie's walkie-talkie out of Officer Doggy's bag, he flipped the machine open and

94

held the transmission button. **KRSSH!**
"Come in! Hello? Sir? Come in." Sally joined
him on the floor, wincing in pain. One of the
infected creatures had attacked her while they
were trying to make their escape. Ben didn't
know a lot about how the Infection worked, but
he knew that he tried to avoid contact with the
Infected whenever he could.

"Are you all right, Sally?" She gave a half-hearted
thumbs-up, clearly the worse for wear. "What were
you doing in a place like this with this Infection
going around?" Ben asked.

"Same thing you are, I'm guessing. Supply runs.
Looking for others. Survivors. Others like us. You
don't know who is on the other side of that walkie-
talkie of yours, do you?"

Ben was about to answer and realized that she was
right. He had been so eager to play hero that he had
never even asked for a name. Sally continued, "I
came here looking for one of my teachers. I was

going to go in, get her, and we were going to get out on a helicopter. The mission went bad, and I got stuck in a room with those animals on the loose." Sally nodded toward Ben. "What about you?"

Ben swallowed dryly. "I was looking for a friend of mine. I *am*—I *am* looking for a friend of mine."

"Well, you've made a new one here," Sally said.

"Thanks, Sally," Ben said appreciatively. In a world like this, you needed all the friends you could get. Sally sat upright. "You know, I think—" **KRSSH!** The static of Ollie's walkie-talkie crackled once more, a familiar posh accent coming through indistinctly on the other end.

"Young man! Young man, are you there?" Ben answered the walkie-talkie by holding down the button on the side. "Yeah, I'm here. And your friend is safe."

"I could have gotten out of there myself!" Sally chimed in.

"Sally, dear! I feared I would never hear from you again!"

"No such luck, boss!" Sally retorted into the walkie-talkie,

"I'm so glad that you were able to find her, young man. Listen to me very carefully now. Just outside the school, there is a Metro station. Take the railway and meet me at the carnival. I have others with me—you will all be safe here."

"I'll see you soon," Sally stated matter-of-factly.

"Oh, I certainly hope so" came the earnest reply. If Sally was annoyed by whoever was on the other end, she didn't show it. Ben really was starting to wonder just who it was that he was helping.

PIGGY:INFECTED

KRSSH! **The signal from the walkie-talkie turned staticky, and Ben tucked the** device back into Doggy's backpack. He helped Sally to her feet, the Infected trapped in the conference room having already fallen asleep once again. The carnival. Ben had lived in Lucella long enough to know of it. But more importantly, for the first time in weeks, he knew what he was doing, where he was going. Renewed vigor coursed through his body, causing him to feel hopeful for the first time in a very long time. After he took Sally to her friend, the man would be so grateful, he would be happy to loan his resources. Ben could look for Ollie for weeks— and he felt as though he already had—and not turn up as much as he could with a helicopter and a few other survivors. Ben couldn't be sure, but he had to imagine that this mysterious benefactor was the only person on the island with a helicopter. When he next went looking for his best friend, it would be with a search party.

Together, Ben and Sally walked down the street, into the night. The fog had rolled in once more, as it seemed to every night, blanketing the city in that same thin layer of mist. The moon shone through the trees, casting a series of eerie shadows on the ground. The wind howled as it blew, chilling the air around them. To the walkie-talkie man's credit, he had been right—the Metro station was just across the street from the school. The two new friends hurried down the steps, Sally hopping effortlessly over the entrance turnstile while Ben slid underneath. The station was huge, an expanse of underground tunnels, a waiting area, several offices, a large cargo room, and an underground storage facility. None of that interested Ben. The train itself sat in the station, its next destination flashing on the overhead boards, but it seemed like this train hadn't moved of its own accord in a while.

"Looks like our ride is here," Ben said sarcastically. "Let's have a look inside." Sally crouched down and offered her palms to Ben, giving him a boost, and he wiggled through the train window, falling inside the train.

Ben used to take the train to school all the time; now the train was hopefully going to take him far away from the school. The irony of it all was not lost on Ben. He didn't have to force his way into the conductor's car—it seemed like the power was still running to the train, which meant it couldn't have been out of order for long. It might even mean that the train still worked. In the conductor's car, Ben saw an open panel, an exposed series of differently shaped gears. He was no engineer, but with the wrench from the conductor's toolbox, he figured he could easily get the train started again. Ben walked back to the passenger area of the train, relaying his plan to Sally.

"Sally! I think we can get this thing up and running again!" She wasn't listening; her eyes were focused on something in the distance.

Ben continued, "Yeah, there's some loose gears in the front car, but if we tighten those up, I think we'll have this thing on the move in no time." Ben would never admit it, to Sally or himself, but he was proud of himself. Not just for his plan to fix the train, but he had been through the wringer the last few weeks, and not only had he survived, he had come out of it with some new skills. "Sally. *Sally?*" Ben peered out of the train again, and that's when he saw them.

The red orbs bouncing in the distance could only mean one thing. More of the Infected. One pair. Two pairs. Four. Six. Ben quickly lost count as the Infected lumbered forward, the cool air blowing in from the outside replaced with the smell of an open old refrigerator. Ben had never seen this many in one place. He flashed back to the fear he felt outside the Lucella Gallery when he had come face-to-face with less than a half dozen. It seemed like every Infected in the city was down here and lumbering toward Sally. He went to

104

open the door of the train for her, but what good would that do them? Packed into a tiny tube underground with nowhere to go, they might as well throw themselves on a buffet line for the Infected. Their horrendous grunting reached a crescendo, a chorus of terrifying grunts as Ben raced back to the conductor's car. His fingers waggled nervously as he threw open the toolbox, grabbing the first wrench he saw. It was the wrong fit, Ben saw almost immediately. He couldn't grip anything inside the control panel, and it wasn't just because of the copious amount of sweat that was suddenly appearing on his hands. Ben wiped his hands on his pants, taking a deep breath to steady himself. It almost never worked, but it was worth a shot. Taking a good look at the conductor's kit and the exposed gears in the control panel, he quickly found the right tool for the job. The cool metal handle of the steel wrench felt especially chilled in his sweaty palms. Wiping a bead of sweat from his brow, Ben ratcheted the wrench around one of the gears, turning it into place. The gear snapped into place with a satisfying clicking sound. He could hear the kerfuffle happening outside, but he did not dare check on it. Every second was precious, and if he didn't get this train moving, it was both of them on the line. Sally had taken out one of the Infected with nothing but an old acorn and a stick—if anyone Ben knew could handle this, it was Sally.

Ben wrenched another gear into place, then a third, and a fourth, finding that the further along he got, the easier the process became. By the time he got to the fifth gear, the thing practically fell away, revealing the throttle and brake for the train. Like most public transportation on the island of Lucella, the train ran on autopilot, but after being locked up, it needed a manual throttling to get it started. Ben threw the throttle into reverse, the train groaning to life as it slowly began to pull away from the station. Signs in different compartments sprang to life, denoting the train's upcoming stops. The carnival grounds were far, but if they hurried, they could definitely make it there by morning. Ben rushed from the front of the car to the middle, where the doors were. They, too, needed to be opened manually, but Ben could see through their windows that the Infected were advancing on Sally.

Ben banged on the doors, to no avail. Sally barely turned, far too busy with the swarm of Infected threatening to overrun her. Latching his wrench onto the door's manual controls, he twisted with all his might, managing to open the doors just enough for Sally to join him on the train. "Sally! Come on! The train is leaving!" **THWACK!** Another acorn arrow right between the eyes of one of the Infected. Sally's aim was always true; her bolts seemed to always hit one of the creatures, stunning them for several long seconds before they recovered and resumed their assault. Maybe the acorns weren't stunning them at all, and the Infected were just as impressed and bewildered as Ben was.

Sally turned to Ben, and he knew what she was going to say before she opened her mouth. "You go on without me. I'll hold them off!"

Ben was horrified by the notion. "Are you kidding me? Come on!"

Sally reloaded her bow with another acorn from Officer Doggy's bag.

"Ben. One of those things got me back at the school. You know it. I know it. But you can still go on. You can still make it. You can find other survivors. You can find your friend . . ."

It wasn't until now that Ben realized just how pale Sally had started to look. The rosy spots on her cheeks had turned sunken, and she appeared sweaty. Looking at her closely, she was certainly much clammier than she had been, even more than when they had left the school. Her hands trembled as she raised her bow again, scoring a hit on an infected Raccoon regardless.

"Look, there's something you need to know about the person you've been talking to—" Sally started, but Ben cut her off.

"You can tell me on the train," Ben insisted, but Sally had already made up her mind.

"No, you *have* to go on without me. I'll stay back and hold off these monsters for as long as I can." He could tell that there was no use arguing with her.

"Well . . . goodbye, Sally." He would have said "See you later," but that seemed cruel. In truth, he did not know.

"Good luck, Ben . . ." Sally trailed off as she raised her bow once more.

Tearing himself away, Ben used the wrench once more, twisting the train doors shut as it began to pick up speed, pulling away from the station. In the distance, he watched Sally get smaller and smaller until she was nothing but a spot, a speck in a background of glowing red eyes. Ben's eyes began to well. His family. Ollie. Officer Doggy. Now Sally. How many people, how many friends was Ben going to lose to this? He dug around in Officer Doggy's pack for the walkie-talkie. Whoever this man was, he was expecting Ben to show up with an old friend. Ben wanted to warn him before he arrived; he would hate to have the man's expectations shattered upon arrival.

KRSSH! "Sir? this is Ben. Come in, sir." **KRSSH!** The plastic device whined with feedback almost immediately, and Ben remembered that even if he wasn't far outside the area where this thing had normally been used, he was currently in an underground tunnel. He would have to wait until he could make it aboveground. Ben made his way to the middle of the train, checking the car for any infected stowaways before throwing Doggy's bag on a seat and lying across the opposite row. He tried to think back to the last time he had gotten a full night's sleep. Maybe that first night in the woods? He had been so exhausted that he had simply passed out. And what had Sally been trying to tell him about her friend? Was all not what it seemed with the mysterious man on the other end of the walkie-talkie? The question plagued his mind as he lay on the cool plastic seat, until the gentle rocking of the train lulled him to sleep.

Ben couldn't have described any of his dreams for the last few nights. The fact that he spent his evenings running from infected versions of his former friends and neighbors was surreal enough for him. He usually dismissed his dreams as soon as he woke. Tonight, he dreamed about Sally, his fervent wishes for her to be okay manifesting in his subconscious. Who was this man on the other end of the walkie-talkie? The question tumbled and turned in his head, and Ben imagined every possibility, every kind of person the man could be, but still felt like he was missing something. Still, he would meet the man in the morning and finally get some answers to his questions. Ben knew that the man would have answers—he just didn't know how, or why. He intended to find out, though. He wouldn't let Sally's and Officer Doggy's sacrifices be in vain. Readjusting himself, Ben went back to sleep. A wise choice. Ben's adventure wasn't over yet, and he would need the rest.

Ben didn't wake until the next evening when the train dinged loudly, lurching to a stop at the carnival grounds. This was the last stop on the train line, and hopefully the last stop on Ben's journey—a journey that had started all that time ago outside Ollie's house. Ben grabbed the conductor's wrench, now his for all intents and purposes—he didn't see the conductor coming back for it—and ratcheted the doors open once again. The Metro carnival ground stop was nowhere near as nice as the one in the city center, but it also didn't seem to have been ravaged by an army of Infected. You took the little victories where you could find them. Decorated signs—depicting high-flying trapeze acts, colorfully painted clowns, and the iconic big top circus image—were plastered all over the Metro station, big blocky arrows pointing in the direction of the carnival grounds.

Ben exited the train, throwing Officer Doggy's bag over his shoulder and tucking the wrench into his pocket. He followed the signs aboveground, moving through the turnstile and continuing up the stairs. The trip had taken longer than he thought, the sun having set over the mountains. *You'd better be ready, sir,* Ben thought to himself, steeled with resolve. *I'm coming for you.* The night air blew lightly over Ben's skin, causing him to pull his now torn and dirty blue hoodie closer around his shoulders. *Tap. Tap. Tap. Tap.* A

red-and-green eye floated in the darkness. Ben had been running for his life long enough to recognize the sound of approaching footsteps. He pulled his wrench from his pocket and brandished it like a weapon. Sure, it wasn't as impressive as a cross-bow, but as someone who had taken more than his fair share of bumps to the noggin since this adventure had begun, Ben knew that even if it wasn't the flashiest weapon, it could still make a lasting impression. The footsteps stopped, just out of sight, hiding in one of the shadows cast by the big tent that housed the main act of the carnival. Ben held a hand to his eyes, trying to get a better look.

"Hey!" Ben shouted toward the shadows. "I'm here to . . ." Ben trailed off as the source of the footsteps stepped out of the shadows. He was a white Badger, roughly Ben's own height, in a pressed white shirt and bright red tie and a pair of dark gray slacks. In his arms, the Badger carried a large vial, its contents glowing almost hypnotically. Ben backed away from him, still holding the wrench defensively. "Uhh . . . who are you?" Ben asked. He didn't claim to possess Officer Doggy's advanced detective skills, but clearly, this person was not the elusive person on the other end of the walkie-talkie.

Another voice called back from within the shadows. "Badgy! Are they infected?"

"I don't think so," yelled back the one they called Badgy, not taking his eyes off Ben, who was—to his credit—still brandishing a plumber's tool like a weapon. "The Infected don't speak, Billy."

"Right. I knew that!" came the reply from the other voice as footsteps joined his partner's in the light. A little taller than Badgy, the one called Billy was a Bull wearing a striped yellow vest and a pair of orange pants. Between his dark gray horns sat a small yellow hard hat. He looked like the kind of Bull who spent a lot of time at the gym. Indeed, while Badgy carried a vial of a mystery substance, Billy carried a barbell, weight plates stacked on

either end. "Please excuse my friend's jadedness; we've had a rough couple of weeks."

"Join the club," Ben shot back, almost bitingly.

"Is there a club?" asked Billy earnestly, his eyes widening. "I really would love to—"

"It's a turn of phrase, Bill," Badgy said, crossing his arms one over the other. "I'm Badgy, and this is my buddy, Billy. Don't try anything funny. In case you hadn't noticed, my friend has a hundred-pound barbell, and he looks strong as a Bull, cuz he is one. So that's two in one."

"I'm Ben." He slowly lowered his wrench but didn't drop his guard. "Are you two here to talk to the man with the helicopter, too?" Badgy and Billy made eye contact for a moment before bursting into laughter so hard, they had to hold each other to remain upright.

"Talk to him?" Badgy cracked up, holding his sides as he doubled over in laughter. "That's a good one. No, we were out here looking for survivors. That's what we do. We have a safe place on the other side of the hill."

"You can come back with us if you like," Billy chimed in. "There's a bunch of us, but there's plenty of room for you and your friend." Maybe Ben hadn't gotten as much rest as he thought. For a moment, he hoped to turn around and find Sally, tired and a little raggedy but otherwise no worse for wear. She would pat him on the shoulder and ask if he'd managed to snag any more of those crunchy acorns from the cafeteria. His hopes were dashed when he turned around, another one of the infected creatures lumbering toward him from the Metro stairs. "That's no friend, Billy. That's one of them!" chirped Badgy. Ben's legs moved before he could form a coherent thought, placing distance between him and the Infected. Badgy and Billy threw themselves in front of him, both drawing their weapons. *"En garde!"*

shouted Badgy as he gripped the vial like a rapier in the tournament fashion, poking and prodding the grunting Infected with the tube, keeping it at bay.

"On guard!" Billy shouted incorrectly as he walloped the infected creature with the end of his barbell, wielding it with an impressive strength.

Stunned, the infected creature's glowing red eyes rolled into the back of its head. Ben gave it another whack with his wrench for good measure. The two survivors led Ben down the alley they had come from, away from the unconscious Infected. Badgy trudged on in silence. Ben couldn't help but notice that Badgy's sleeve had been torn in the scuffle, his arm glowing the same color as the liquid in the vial he carried. Billy had fared much better; there was hardly a scratch on him, and he continued to lift his barbell as they walked as if he feared he might miss some exercise goal that had been set for him. Boosting one another up

onto a dumpster, the trio climbed up a fire escape, leading them to the roofs of Lucella. The moon cast an eerie light over the city, still beautiful from this high up. Badgy noticed Ben's gaze.

"You ever seen the island like this?" he queried.

"No," Ben answered truthfully. He had never seen the island like this before, and in more ways than one. He looked up at the moon, shining down across the city, and briefly wondered if Ollie was out there somewhere looking at the same night sky, wondering about the same moon.

"What were you doing before all this?" Badgy asked as they traipsed along the rooftops.

"I was looking for someone. A friend of mine. What about you?"

Badgy drew his tattered jacket around his shoulders, the glowing arm catching the light of the moon and the mysterious green shade catching the light of the moon in all the right ways. He looked at it wistfully, as though suddenly remembering a long forgotten past.

"I was a research assistant. Oh, the wonders of science. The things we were doing. The things we were close to—" Badgy caught himself, finishing with an exhalation and letting out a sigh of relief. "I'm glad that I can help people find safety. I couldn't imagine losing anyone to the Infection." Ben's eyes fell to the ground. He didn't have to imagine it. The Infection had controlled his entire life for the last few weeks. Billy chimed in, hoping to save the conversation from its awkward turn.

"I was studying to be a bodybuilder, like my father." Billy interjected. "How did you make it all the way to the carnival grounds?" Billy queried. "You said that you were looking for someone?" The question wasn't out of line; Ben was pretty far from home at this point. He answered as honestly as he could.

"I have to see whoever the man on the other end of this walkie-talkie is. If we're lucky, he knows something about what's going on with this Infection."

"Well, all right, Ben. You should at least stay here with us for a little while," Billy offered. "We can help you find the person you're looking for. Hey, maybe that's him!" Badgy and Ben lifted their heads, eyes following Billy's gesture. Atop a roof on the opposite side of the street was the shady character from the gallery. A hood still obscured their face.

"That guy's been following since before I left the city," Ben murmured, loud enough for Badgy and Billy to hear him.

"Why?" Badgy asked quizzically.

Again, Ben answered as honestly as his knowledge of the situation would allow. "I don't know."

"Well, there's only one way to find out," Billy enthused, racing across the rooftops. Ben took off after him, and Badgy, exasperated, followed. There was nowhere for the hooded man to run, not with three of the survivors bearing down on him. Leaping to another nearby rooftop, the hooded man slid down the fire escape and took off running down the alleyway.

"And we're sure he isn't one of them?" Billy asked as he made his way down the same fire escape.

"The Infected don't run away from people, Billy. They don't run at all."

"He's right," Ben agreed. "They kind of . . . lurch."

"I would have said that they 'stagger,'" Billy offered.

"That's a good one, too. Look! He's going into that mall!" Badgy directed as, sure enough, the hooded figure threw open the doors to the mall and entered.

"He ran this way!" Billy announced, but Ben still had questions.

"A mall? Why would they hide here?" That summed up this adventure for Ben. Every time he got a new answer, he was presented with a baker's dozen of additional questions. The trio followed, throwing the doors to the mall open again, and chasing the hooded man.

It took Ben's eyes a while to adjust to the inside of the mall. These were the brightest lights he had seen in a while. He stepped through the metal detector at the entrance without issue, even with the hammer and wrench. Billy and his hundred-pound, five-foot-long stainless-steel barbell didn't have it as easy. The machine blared. If they had been aiming for the element of surprise, they had certainly lost it. Billy lifted his barbell with one hand, bringing it down on the machine repeatedly until the blaring devolved into a sad trumpeting sound, then stopped altogether. He stepped sideways through the machine. Though Ben was sure that no one had been in here for weeks, the mall was still running like it was seeing its old level of activity. The dozens of food stalls on the first floor had long since shuttered, but Ben could smell the cuisine still wafting through the air. He couldn't remember the last time he'd had a mall pretzel, and now he could barely think of anything else. Almost. There was still the matter of the hooded man, who was, at this moment, making his way up the massive escalator at the center of the mall. Either he was headed for the second floor—Men's Casual Wear and Birdy Bank—or he was trying to escape.

Billy and Ben made a beeline for the escalators. The flashing lights and sounds in the mall made Ben feel like he was in a video game, but he knew in his heart that a video game about an Infection apocalypse could never be made. Some things were better as real stories. Maybe someday, Ben would come back and try his luck at the Aye-Aye

Arcade, but right now, he had far more pressing issues. Billy and Ben launched up the escalator, hot on the hooded man's tail. Badgy took the stairs, and with an almost-imperceptible movement, Badgy used his claws to cut down a banner, the hanging advertisement for Kitty's Kitchen, which began falling down in front of the hooded man. The hooded man tripped over the sign, every attempt to free himself resulting in tangling himself further in the banner. Badgy stood over the hooded man, admiring his handiwork. If Ben had any doubts about his skills, they left the moment Badgy put his boot on the hooded man's chest, mysterious glowing vial pointed at his face.

"No, no, no! Please don't hurt me! Please, I'm just a kid!"

Ben's brow furrowed, every emotion he had bottled up for the last few weeks rising to the surface immediately and threatening to boil over. Tears welled in his eyes as he nodded at Badgy. Using the glowing vial, he flipped the man's hood off his face, revealing his Catlike features and immediately confirming Ben's new suspicions.

"Ollie?!" Ben shouted, his voice cracking with emotion. It was as if the air had been sucked out of the room. Ben fell to his knees, pulling Ollie out of the banner and into a tight embrace. He never wanted to let his friend go. Ben pressed his face into the crook of his friend's neck, letting the tears

flow freely now. It seemed like so long ago that he had stood outside Ollie's house, wondering where his friend had gone. So long now since that first Infected had knocked him out and dragged him inside. So long since he had escaped and ran to the police station. Everything Ben had done for the last several weeks—every fight he had been in, every muscle ache, every sleepless night—had been to find his friend, and now he had. Now he could rest. Ben's fingers curled into a fist, and he punched his friend hard in the arm.

"Do you know how long I've been looking for you?"

"Ummm . . . No?" Ollie replied truthfully.

"I . . . ! You . . . ! Everything I've done . . . !" It wasn't an eloquent retelling of the last few weeks, but it would have to do until Ben could gather his thoughts.

"Why did you run?" Badgy asked, obviously much more put together than Ben was at the moment. Ben nodded in agreement—that was a good question.

"Are you kidding me? All I've been doing for months is running," Ollie replied, beginning to extricate himself from the banner. "A few weeks ago, my family visited the hospital. But after their visit, they started acting weird. And scary. I came to this part of the island looking for my grandma, but when I got here, everyone was acting weird and scary, so I hid. I've been looking out for the Infected and watching for survivors ever since. The only problem is, you can't tell the difference until it's too late."

"Well, any friend of Ben's is a friend of ours," Billy said cheerfully, helping Ollie to his feet. "You ought to come with us. You'll be well taken care of at The Safe Place." Ollie nodded in appreciation, taking his hood down to wipe his teary eyes.

"Will I ever see my family again?" For a moment, there was no answer.

"Let's get going," Badgy said, taking charge and leaving the question hanging in the air. The truth was, there was no way of knowing. Would any of them ever see their families again, and if so . . . what would that even look like?

"I wish some of these food stalls were open. I haven't had Kitty's Kitchen in forever. I wonder if they still serve those butter bites," Billy moaned as they passed a particularly delicious-smelling stall.

"How can you even think about eating at a time like this?" Badgy wondered aloud.

"Don't act like I didn't hear your stomach growling while we were chasing the mallrat," Billy shot back with a chuckle. "It was the loudest thing I've ever heard!"

Badgy tucked his mystery vial back into his jacket. "You must be mistaken. Unlike some of us, I never patrol on an empty stomach."

"Yeah, right, Badge. Then what was that grunting sound I heard back there?"

Badgy froze in place, realizing what was happening just a second before everyone else. At the bottom of the steps, three infected creatures lay in wait, each armed with a wooden plank of some sort. Another three Infected stood at the bottom of the escalator, lurching forward, only to be pushed back as they attempted to come up the descending escalator.

"It's them . . ." Ollie whispered, his voice a mixture of fascination and pure dread. I never had the time to take a good look at them before.

"Lucky" came the reply in triplicate from Ben, Badgy, and Billy, each arming themselves for battle once more. Billy hefted his barbell. Ben

drew the conductor's wrench from his backpack. Badgy's vial glowed as he waved it back and forth.

"Seriously, what is that thing?" Ben finally queried.

"That's actually a great story," Badgy replied. "I'll tell it to you someday if we get out of here." Looking at his friends, Ollie put up his fists. No, Ben had already lost Ollie for too long. It was his job now to make sure that Ollie was protected. A crowbar lay next to an automated transaction machine, the remnants of an obvious and futile attempt to rob this place. Sure, bring out the robot with a chain-saw arm for a break-in, but an invasion of an Infected army? Though the heist may have failed, that didn't make it a total loss. Ben grabbed the crowbar and handed it Ollie. "You see anyone that isn't me, Badgy, or Billy, you start swinging, okay?" Ollie nodded, wrapping his fingers around the cool metal handle of the crowbar.

"This is Badgy and Billy, by the way; they're friends of mine."

Badgy and Billy waved as best they could as they held their weapons. The Infected seemed to have figured out the stairs. While on the ground, the Infected were slow and unwieldy; when it came to stairs, they seemed to almost glide up them, bringing their horrible odor and attitude for violence with them. Badgy and Billy went to work immediately, and Ben could see how the duo had managed to survive together for so long. Badgy was all finesse; he would dip, dive, and duck in and out of the fight, avoiding or countering any move that the Infected could throw at him. He even managed to disarm one of them. Billy seemed to be less inclined to demonstrate finesse and was much more interested in . . . well, walloping the Infected with his giant barbell. Every time one of them would lunge for Badgy and inevitably miss, Billy was there to smack the Infected on the side of the head with a resounding thud. It never took them out of the fight for more than half a minute, but when you had been fighting infected creatures for as long as Ben assumed these two had, sometimes that was all you needed.

For their part, Ben and Ollie helped take out the escalator Infected, a much simpler task, given that this group of Infected still hadn't figured out which way the escalator worked yet. They shuffled in line, each one only getting a few steps onto the escalator before it deposited them back at the beginning. Ollie and Ben took them out with wild abandon. Ollie in particular was taking to the crowbar like a duck to water. There wasn't much to swinging a crowbar, but to Ben, Ollie was making it look like a long-lost art form. Having stunned or dispatched the rest of the Infected, Badgy and Billy joined the two separated friends at the bottom of the stairs. Luckily for the quartet, exits at the mall were clearly marked. What Ben wouldn't have given to have this kind of signage back at the school or the Lucella Gallery.

The group passed a shuttered sporting goods shop—Ben couldn't help but think how much Sally would have loved to break in and pick up a new crossbow. They could use her marksmanship and her optimism right now. Following the exit signage, the group were finally able to find the back entrance—boarded over, of course, with over a dozen wooden planks. They had most likely been placed there long ago to keep the Infected out, but it was becoming clear that they were doing more to keep them in.

"I've got this," Billy declared boldly, discarding his barbell and taking several steps back. Getting a running start, he lowered his head toward the planks and promptly bounced off them. It seemed that, hardheaded as he may be, the wooden planks had been placed there by a professional and had no intention of being smashed apart.

"I could probably help . . ." came Ollie's tiny voice as he presented his crowbar. It seemed the small metal bar was good for something other than breaking tokens out of machines. Ollie pressed the bar between the wall and the wooden board, using the entirety of his not-substantial body weight to crack one of the wooden boards in half. It snapped loudly, splintering in the middle as Badgy reached down and removed it, with Ollie ready to take off the next one. This board also snapped in half, the cracking sound echoing down the hallway, surely drawing in Infected who had only been stunned and were now angry. Another piece of the wooden barricade came off as Ollie pried the wooden bars off the door.

"Okay, but I loosened it for you," Billy said sheepishly.

The Infected were advancing on them. Ben had been through this so many times in the last few weeks, he felt no fear, only urgency. The sooner they got out of here, the sooner they could get to The Safe Place and debate their next move. If Ben had any say in it, they would be headed straight for the man who had been communicating on channel 2. Ollie was moving faster now, prying off the top of the boards and letting Badgy and Billy handle the rest. Just in time, they pulled the last board off the door, Billy throwing it at the nearest Infected. It hit the thing's head with a dull *BONK*, but the Infected barely seemed to notice. The quartet pushed through the doors, shutting them behind them. Ollie relinquished his crowbar, stuffing it into the door handles to barricade it. Ollie had always been a smart kid—maybe that was how he had survived in Lucella all this time.

The group composed themselves, with Badgy leading the way. Ben was used to leading the way, but this far from home, he felt especially useless. He hoped that this Safe Place was as nice as Billy had described it, but he didn't particularly care. For the last few weeks, he'd slept on train seats and fallen logs. His back hurt. His feet hurt. His head hurt. However, all that was eclipsed by the fact that he had done it, he had finally done it. He had found Ollie. Ben shot a look over at his friends, happy to have found any of them, let alone three of them.

They walked until dawn. Just as the sun began to peek over the island, spilling a warm glow over the city, Billy took a deep breath of fresh air and exhaled. The fog that seemed to plague the island pulled back in the mornings, leaving it covered with a fresh layer of dew. Maybe it was because Ben had not been out at night for so long, but it felt as though it made the air crisper. Or maybe all the air Ben had been breathing was recycled and stained with the stench of the Infected. It was hard to tell anymore.

"Home, safe home!" Billy announced, gesturing ahead of them with a low, sweeping bow. Ben let a

small smile crack his usually stern visage for the first time in days.

The Safe Place, as it had been deemed colloquially by its residents, was the biggest building that Ben had ever seen in real life. From the outside, Ben could count at least five stories, and if Billy was to be believed, there were multiple bedrooms, storage rooms, a radio room, a gym, a cafeteria, and laundry. Ben looked down at his favorite hoodie, ragged from weeks of use—snagging on branches, being dragged across pavement, stains whose origins Ben didn't even want to ponder. The idea of doing laundry delighted Ben for the first time in his life.

Zero. Zero. Zero. Zero. Ben watched Billy type in the code for the gate, the massive chain-link fence pulling back as Billy entered the correct password. Simple, and easy to remember, and it wasn't as if any of the Infected were using touch pads. If wooden blocks were enough to keep people inside,

Ben figured that a locked gate would be more than enough to keep them outside. The gate creaked open just enough to let the quartet inside before a pulley system sent it back the other way, shutting it again.

"Badgy! Badgy! Badgy! Badgy!" Ben dug in his ear with his finger, sure that he was not hearing things in stereo.

"My girls!" Badgy yelled, bending down to receive the two little rockets who launched themselves at him, tackling him to the ground. As he stood, the two young children launched themselves at Badgy again, who playfully fought them off.

"At ease, Silver Paws!" The children straightened up immediately, standing in formation. The booming command came from a gray Wolf at the end of the hall. She wore a black jacket and a purple shirt, a black combat scarf draped around her neck. "What's all this commotion?"

"Badgy's back!" the two shouted in unison. They might not look exactly alike, but really were on the exact same wavelength, mannerisms and all. "And he brought friends!" For the first time, Ben saw Badgy crack a genuine smile as he hugged the two tightly before standing up and gesturing to Ben and Ollie. "Willow, this is Ben, and this is Ollie. It's making a long story short, but we found them wandering around the carnival grounds and then the mall."

"You *look* funny," the kids blurted, peeking out at Ben from their position of salute.

"Okay, well, umm . . . thank you," Ben replied.

"TSP—dismissed!" barked Willow. The two younger children broke rank, disappearing into the hubbub of The Safe Place.

"TSP. The Safe Place! You're the ones who have been leaving notes all over the city!"

"Oh, you've seen those, huh? You must get around. If you're going to stay here, you have to sign in." Willow produced a clipboard for him to sign in on. "TSP isn't The Safe Place—it's The Silver Paws. An organization founded near the beginning of the outbreak. I was once a thief, but when I got out of jail, I started recruiting survivors, starting with my closest friends. We set up shop where we could; the Lucella Oil Farms, factories in the heart of the island. Every time we raise a new settlement, we leave notes for any other survivors to come join us." Ben nodded as he took the sign-up sheet from her, two names immediately jumping out at him. No, they couldn't be. Not here? "Badgy. Billy. It's good to have you back. We've been debating what to do with this information until you returned."

"Oh, heck. What is it?" asked Badgy, cocking his head at the files Willow was holding in her hands. Willow cleared her throat, causing the whiskers on the side of her face to twinge.

"You see, Badgy, it's just that this is . . . sensitive information." Willow hemmed and hawed, eyes remaining focused on Ben and Ollie. They were outsiders, and whatever she had to say was too precious to let others hear.

"Anything you can say in front of me and Billy, you can say in front of Ben and Ollie. They've proven themselves a dozen times over tonight." Badgy nodded at Ben and Ollie, and Ben nodded back. Trust was a rare commodity in a world where everyone on the other side of the fence was just as likely to try to eat you as take you in.

"Very well," Willow continued. "We've been hearing it for weeks, but we couldn't put a source to it until recently." Willow flipped open the file folder in her hands, a series of photos boasting blurry images of a helicopter.

"It's a helicopter," Willow explained, as though that weren't obvious from the pictures they were being shown. "We think it belongs to—"

"Him . . ." Ben finished the sentence. He remembered hearing about the mysterious man's helicopter and thinking that the man sounded like the only person on the island who had one. It looked like his theory was proving itself correct.

"It's been flying overhead every day for a couple of days now," Willow continued, "but we just managed to get a tracker on its signal last night. That means—"

"We can find out where it's coming from, and where it's going," Badgy mused, cutting Willow off. Badgy turned to Ben, as if waiting for his decision. It was a no-brainer.

"I need to go and see him," Ben stated matter-of-factly. For Officer Doggy. For *Sally*.

"Well, that settles it," declared Badgy. "You're going, and Billy and I are coming with you."

"Nooo!" groaned a number of the younger TSP agents. The kids from earlier appeared as if from nowhere, each contorting their faces into incredible pouts, crocodile tears welling in their eyes. Badgy bent down to their level as well as he could.

"I'll be back soon, I promise. And have I ever broken a promise to you two?"

"Nooo . . ." the TSP agents groaned as they slowly extricated themselves from his legs.

Badgy stood them next to each other. "Take care of Ollie while we're gone."

Ollie's jaw dropped. "Wait, I'm not coming? Ben . . . Ben, tell them I'm coming!" Honestly Ben wished that his friend could. But he had just gotten Ollie back, after he had accepted the fact that he might never see him again. What kind of friend would Ben be, putting Ollie back in that danger? And if he had seen what he thought he had seen on the registry, he wanted everyone that he cared about in one place, far away from the Infected.

"Stay here, Ollie. I'll be back soon, I promise."
He echoed Badgy's words to the TSP because he
couldn't think of any comforting words of his
own. He wondered how many times he could
escape the wrath of the Infected before his luck
ran out. He only needed the one more time.
Slinging Officer Doggy's bag over his shoulder,
he sidled up alongside Badgy and Billy, the gate
cranking open once more.

The Safe Place was generous enough to let them
use a truck, its bed piled high with things they
might need on their journey. Ben hadn't bothered to look, but if the place was as nice as Billy
seemed to think it was, he was sure that they
would have all the supplies they needed. The
kids ran around the base of the gate as they
departed. Ollie was nowhere to be seen. Maybe
saying goodbye was too hard for him, but at least
he was safe.

161

Badgy, Ben, and Billy spent most of the drive just talking. About who they were, who they wanted to be, who they would have been if it weren't for this Infection. For the first time in a long time, Ben let himself relax in the company of friends. Not unlike on the train in the Metro, it wasn't long before the rhythmic rocking of the vehicle put Ben to sleep. This time, his sleep was mercifully dreamless. No red-eyed Infected bearing down on him, no puzzles that he had to solve to escape a room, no multicolored keys to collect. It was a sleep so peaceful that it was almost suspicious. The truck pulled to a stop, and Ben arose, hopping out of the back and stretching his body. It was night again, though this time, no fog hung over the city. For the first time in days, Ben had spent the better part of the last few months thinking that everything that could happen to him had the highest stakes possible, but looking up at the stars with his friends, he suddenly felt like a very small part of something much bigger.

"So this is where the signal leads," Billy said, holding up a touchscreen tablet with a large blinking red dot on it. "You can thank the finest state-of-the-art technology for that one." Wordlessly Badgy pointed to his left. In the middle of the field sat a helicopter, propellers spinning gently in the cool night breeze. "Yeah, sure, I guess you could use your eyes, too, like a Neanderthal."

"Keep your eyes peeled," Badgy advised. "I've never been to this side of the island. I have no idea what to expect. As long as we don't get taken by surprise, we should be fine."

"Oof!" came a voice from behind them, causing the trio to jump. Badgy drew the vial from beneath his jacket with almost frightening speed, pointing it toward the source of the sound. He drew his arm back, poking the vial into the bags in the backseat of the car. "Yow!" exclaimed Ollie as he hopped out of the back, holding his backside in pain.

"Ollie?" Ben asked, surprised. "What are you doing here? Aren't The Silver Paws watching you?"

Ollie pulled a long baseball bat from where he had been hiding. "No way. Thanks to you, it was not easy to ditch those guys. There's two of them. I found this old bat in the gym and I figured it would be perfect for a grand *slam*."

"How are you going to win all four tennis championships with a baseball bat?" Billy queried.

"He means the baseball one," Badgy interjected. "It's where you hit a home run with all the bases loaded."

"Thank you," Ollie told Badgy.

"I don't care what sport you're playing—you're going to wait in the truck," Ben said, putting his foot down. "I can't believe you stowed away."

"Hey! Whatever this is, the person down there might know something about what happened to my family. I want to see them."

"And it looks like you're not the only one," Billy mused, pointing behind the two friends. A sight that Ben was getting all too familiar seeing—a horde of infected creatures—was on the march toward them. Ben couldn't see how many there were, just the throng of floating red eyes in the distance. Badgy held up his touchscreen tablet once more, punching in a few commands. The screen shifted, and a green dot appeared right next to them, corresponding with a laboratory. "That's where you're going to want to go. Whatever is in this lab, it's going to have the answers you need. Take Ollie in there with you. Billy and I will hold them off." Billy nodded solemnly, lifting his giant barbell from the back of the truck, its plates clanking into place. "Gentlemen . . . it's been an honor."

Ben didn't want to leave his new friends. Not again. But if he didn't get to the bottom of this mystery, he didn't want to think about how many more friends he might have to leave behind . . . or be left behind himself. Officer Doggy and Sally didn't deserve their fates. Maybe they were still out there, part of a traveling group of ragtag survivors. The thought admittedly did put a smile on Ben's face, but one that he couldn't afford to share. When he was back at The Safe Place with Ollie, Badgy, and Billy, with Willow barking orders and TSP running around, when he was reunited with his family—that was when he would allow himself some time to just . . . be himself. Right now there was too much at stake. He pulled Ollie toward the lab.

On the crest of the hill, an army of the Infected made its way toward Badgy and Billy. The moonlight glinted off Badgy's vial as he thrusted and parried, warming himself up for the battle that he knew was about to take place. His very life was at stake, and with it, Billy's life, the lives of Willow, the TSP agents, and everyone at The Safe Place. If this was their last stand, Badgy would have to be sensational. Billy's barbells had never been quite as flashy as Badgy's mystery vial, but Billy had never needed it to be. It was two pieces of steel, with a steel beam in the middle, an instrument that had served him quite well in the past. Every chip, every dent told a story, a story that he had lived to share. He convinced himself that today was no different. He hoped that he was right. As the Infected began to climb the hill toward them, Billy spoke. "Badgy . . . If we don't make it out of this, I just want to let you know . . ." Billy trailed off, but it wasn't necessary.

"I already know, Billy" came Badgy's gentle reply. In the distance, Ben swore he heard Badgy's voice echoing across the night. "En garde!"

Ben wasn't sure if there was a protocol in a situation like this. Months ago, he would have just been happy to find Ollie. Or The Safe Place. Finding both of them was beyond his wildest dreams. Yet here he was, possibly giving up his chance at keeping both his best friend and a found family for the one thing that neither of those things could provide for him. Answers. Ben raised his hand, rapping on the door of the laboratory. He waited a moment for an answer. It would be just his luck if he had gone all this way to find an empty laboratory. He had seen the helicopter parked outside; he knew someone was here. He raised his fist again, knuckles falling on thin air as the door whooshed open before he could knock again. Whoever was here, they were expecting him. Ben turned to Ollie, and Ollie nodded solemnly, raising his new baseball bat above his shoulders, ready for a grand slam in whatever form it took. It had been a long journey for the both of them, but nevertheless they stepped into the lab, content in knowing that whatever they found, they would face it together.

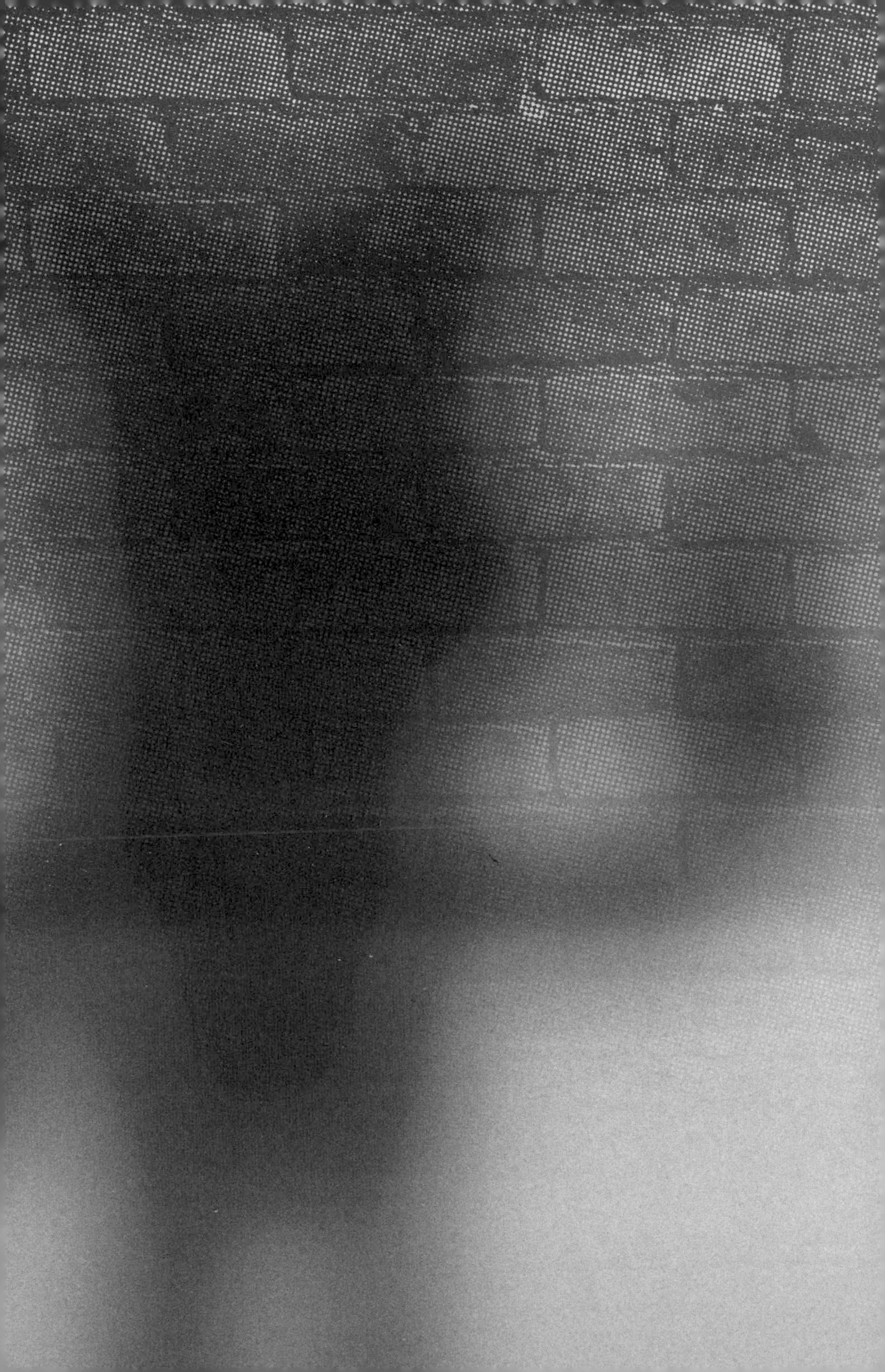

About the Author and Illustrator

Terrance Crawford is a humor and pop culture writer from Detroit, Michigan, who lives in New York, New York. At the time of printing, he still has not received his Hogwarts letter.

Dan Widdowson is a children's illustrator from Loughborough, England. He graduated from the Arts University Bournemouth in 2014 and has been working on children's illustration projects with The Bright Agency ever since. With a keen interest in storytelling and narrative, Dan is working toward bringing his own picture books to life in the near future.